Artists

ARTISTS

A NOVEL

ANDREW GROF

SUNSTONE PRESS

SANTA FE

Sunstone books may be purchased for educational, business, or sales promotional use. For information please write: Special Markets Department, Sunstone Press, P.O. Box 2321, Santa Fe, New Mexico 87504-2321.

Book and cover design › Vicki Ahl
Body typeface › Goudy Old Style MT
Printed on acid-free paper
∞
eBook 978-1-61139-486-3

Library of Congress Cataloging-in-Publication Data

Names: Grof, Andrew, 1946- author.
Title: Artists : a novel / by Andrew Grof.
Description: Santa Fe, New Mexico : Sunstone Press, [2016]
Identifiers: LCCN 2016035407 (print) | LCCN 2016040987 (ebook) | ISBN 9781632931450 (softcover : alk. paper) | ISBN 9781611394863
Classification: LCC PS3607.R6343 A89 2016 (print) | LCC PS3607.R6343 (ebook) | DDC 813/.6--dc23
LC record available at https://lccn.loc.gov/2016035407

SUNSTONE PRESS IS COMMITTED TO MINIMIZING OUR ENVIRONMENTAL IMPACT ON THE PLANET. THE PAPER USED IN THIS BOOK IS FROM RESPONSIBLY MANAGED FORESTS. OUR PRINTER HAS RECEIVED CHAIN OF CUSTODY (COC) CERTIFICATION FROM: THE FOREST STEWARDSHIP COUNCIL™ (FSC®), PROGRAMME FOR THE ENDORSEMENT OF FOREST CERTIFICATION™ (PEFC™), AND THE SUSTAINABLE FORESTRY INITIATIVE® (SFI®).
THE FSC® COUNCIL IS A NON-PROFIT ORGANIZATION, PROMOTING THE ENVIRONMENTALLY APPROPRIATE, SOCIALLY BENEFICIAL AND ECONOMICALLY VIABLE MANAGEMENT OF THE WORLD'S FORESTS. FSC® CERTIFICATION IS RECOGNIZED INTERNATIONALLY AS A RIGOROUS ENVIRONMENTAL AND SOCIAL STANDARD FOR RESPONSIBLE FOREST MANAGEMENT.

WWW.SUNSTONEPRESS.COM
SUNSTONE PRESS / POST OFFICE BOX 2321 / SANTA FE, NM 87504-2321 /USA
(505) 988-4418 / ORDERS ONLY (800) 243-5644 / FAX (505) 988-1025

For Caryl

"Nothing is more real than nothing."
     —Democritus as translated by Beckett

"Failure is absolute."
                    —Anonymous

It all starts with light, with colors.

My very first memories of light and colors in my father's studio, and this before all shapes and substances, the light filtered and the colors blended before I managed to separate them in my mind, I was thought a backward, a slow-witted child, throughout my young years I was examined by a number of specialists who diagnosed various maladies of the body and the spirit, but this coupled with a kind of restlessness released me from all remedies recommended by the so-called experts.

My mistrust of words even then.

I drew incessantly, my father and I communicated through drawings and sketches, things seen as well as imagined, in time I became his best audience and he mine.

My father something of a dandy back then.

With his cane and top hat he appeared a creature from another time and place, unlike others in my life he could never be mistaken for anyone but himself, he carried himself with an unsmiling seriousness that appeared to negate the very passage of time, the very solidity of the man created through an exaggerated simplicity and exactitude of movements and gestures, which is not to say he was humorless but his humor issued from deep within with few if any outward signs, although this kind, his peculiar kind of humor now and again made him appear as light as air to my eyes.

My hands, my fingers arthritic now.

I once toyed with the idea of writing all this down, but now I couldn't even if I wanted to which I never seriously did.

Memory sufficient for my needs, my purposes. I follow its meandering ways the way one follows a river across changing terrains, now slow, now fast, crooked then straight, thoughts now birthing negating then once more birthing other thoughts, I both watch and listen as though I were watching and listening to someone else, someone I once was but no longer am.

For most of his life my father worked, created his art in the city.

"I am no artist," he once told me. "Never call me, mistake me for one. All art, all artists nothing but fakes, the so-called business of art nothing but the business of fakery, of pulling the wool over people's eyes, of telling them what to see and think when they are perfectly capable of seeing and thinking on their own. I am simply a worker in light and colors, I have no designs on anyone, not even myself."

Our so-called conversations one-way affairs, my father talked and I listened, his words then as if intended for himself, for to the end of his life he was never quite certain how much I grasped, was capable of comprehending, he played it safe, simply talked out loud to himself and hoped for the best.

It was only towards the end of his life he moved to the country, to his dacha in the country, leaving his art, any and all reminders of his so-called art behind but taking me with him of course, for given my questionable, unstable condition where and how was I to survive on my own.

"The city's become impossible," he told me, told himself. "The noise, the movement all from without, from the very first a city sets out to destroy, to replace all space and silence within with its own density and noise, it's only someone who is both willing and capable of forgetting, of surrendering who and what he is that can exist, survive in a city, a city with nothing to offer and everything to steal, survival from one week, day, hour to the next the only possible option, like Cronus a city does nothing more than eat and digest its own children," and here he made a reference to one of Goya's drawings with which I was familiar, "its hunger, its greed is insatiable, it won't stop until it will have turned all the living into the dead with the dead all alike, indistinguishable one from the other, it's only the living that exemplify the uniqueness of life, and the city can't abide the living, only the dead."

As if to interrupt the flow of his words occasionally my father seized me by the shoulders and stared deep into my eyes as if hoping to make some sort of contact beyond words or looking for himself perhaps, his mirror image in my eyes.

"Only the struggles of the heart worth the effort," he finished. "Leave the struggles of the intellect to those who only live in the intellect, to city dwellers who don't mind dying, being consumed by others and themselves."

In the city we spent much of our time in museums.

To avoid the crowds we went either early in the morning or late at night and never on weekends, my father walking with the determined steps of an explorer moving through the passageways of time, it was up to me to keep up, never to lose sight of his bulky frame in our progress, now and again I feared becoming irretrievably lost in Pharaoh's tombs or the Virgin's reconstructed cathedrals, my father always moving forward and never back, his steps as if predetermined, carefully planned out in advance.

"We're entering the Quattrocento," he would occasionally stop and ponderously announce, or the Renaissance or returning to the Caves of Lascaux. A slight pause, always a slight pause after leaving one period and entering another, like divers ascending from certain depths we meant to avoid the confusing, the deleterious effects of the bends. My father my scout, my guide. These journeys into the past would have been unimaginable without him.

Each period, each phase of so-called human artistic productivity demanded its own pace and ways of looking. At times we moved along with measured steps while at others my father hurried us along as if to escape the hold of a particular place and period. But in each epoch, my father unfailingly called them epochs, we always paused in front of one or two so-called representative works of art, in fact sat down in front of a number of so-called works of art with my father as if frozen in concentration, lost to me I felt and to himself as well perhaps.

The demands of certain paintings, sculptures at times more than he could handle I feared.

"Enter," he spoke without gesturing or even raising his hand, "now and again you must enter a work as if at your own risk, like entering life itself, the artist demands not just your eyes, your presence but your very being, your soul itself. You're on your own then. You may enter or not, but if you enter there are no guarantees you'll exit sane and whole, exit the same person you were on entering."

It was only years later, in fact long after my father's death that I began to have an inkling of just what he had been talking about, at the time I was too uncertain and frightened to surrender myself the way he seemed able to himself.

"The best artists, the best so-called workers in art are not at all concerned with the way the world is or even as it should be, for that any hack with the least bit of talent is more than sufficient, no, their concern is both appearance and world denying, they are after some inner light or truth," and he pronounced "truth" in a slow, drawn-out fashion as if it didn't even belong with the other words, "which can be seized only gradually and with a great deal of effort, and then, no, not seized at all but only suggested, hinted at, in other words their very success as so-called great artists depends on their failure as artists in the ordinary sense, in other words they can hardly be said to succeed until they fail and fail miserably and in a most provocative fashion in the eyes of ordinary onlookers, but those, yes, only those so-called artists are worthy of true study and real penetration, just as we ourselves without our realizing it are worthy of true study and deep penetration."

My head was swimming. In his very revelations my father only succeeding in confusing, in leaving me behind.

"In general the world satisfied with so little," he continued. "They mean only to be cuddled, reassured, just listen to the comments of the people passing by, 'How interesting,' or, 'Isn't that interesting,' they all begin, they abhor the silence that would come from true looking, from deep penetration, they want nothing to do with challenges but only with assurances and reassurances, the last thing they want is to penetrate the very depths of their true miseries and joys, to stand face to face with themselves in front of a so-called great work of art, they simply mean to talk their way through life until they fall into the most unnatural silence through decrepitude or loss of energy, never in their entire lives do they distinguish between what is important and unimportant, real and unreal, like certain schools of fish they are perfectly content swimming near the surface regardless of the dangers involved, they lack both the desire as well as the ability to dive deep to see what they might discover."

Yes, I nodded, yes.

Not because I understood but because of the usual mesmerizing effect of my father's words which once begun I didn't want to stop, like riding certain waves whose origins and very nature are baffling to our senses.

"You look serious," my father suddenly looked at me. "Don't be. Seriousness the greatest obstacle to real understanding, the shallowest, the most insipid individuals wear seriousness like a shield, an armor, they mistakenly protect themselves against the nakedness of the very real absurdity and humor of life itself."

We always made it a point to dine at the museum cafeterias, where in the general din of crashing utensils and snatches of conversation my father continued his musings.

"Being so-called objective is the hardest, the most difficult thing in life. How can we possibly be given the subjective beings that we are, we view everything including ourselves through our subjective lenses, tell ourselves that our very survival depends on nothing less than our particular and peculiar subjectivities, to be truly objective is a real impossibility which is what makes it all important, the possible never that important, only the impossible ever is."

I had tuna on rye and my father the fruit salad.

He chewed his food with the same care and attention reserved for his words which I tried to imitate in vain, I took large bites, chunks of food which I greedily swallowed in preparation for the next bite and the one after.

"We become artists," my father continued, "not because we want to reproduce the world but because we mean to escape it. In the same way we become so-called artists, and I'm talking of serious artists, not because we want to duplicate, to reproduce ourselves but because we mean to escape it. Only second, third and fifth rate artists are endlessly concerned with so-called expressing themselves, creating endless births and rebirths for themselves when their first, their original birth should have been more than sufficient. No. So-called true, so-called first rate artists become artists in order to negate, to leave themselves behind, nothing but nothing matters to them except this loss, this denial of the self," and here he reached across the table to keep me from chewing, swallowing too fast, "the only problem is, and it's a huge, a magnificent, an insoluble one, that the more intent they are on losing themselves the more they begin to assert themselves, that is in time and through time in their so-called art they do nothing but assert themselves, render themselves visible through their art in spite of their feeling, no, knowing the self to be the greatest obstacle to true creativity, in the end they paint or sculpt themselves into a trap from which there is no escape, they find themselves at the mercy of their art instead of the other way around, which is why so many artists, so-called great artists wind up killing themselves, art no longer a means of escape for them, death, yes, death the only option."

Did I fear for my father then and so for myself as well?

He must have read something of this in my face, for no sooner had he finished saying what he had than he hastened to reassure me that this was not, could never be the case with him. "Rest assured, Martin, I am not nor did I ever set out to be a so-called great artist, the traps all too visible from the start, which is why I was and always will be simply a worker in art, a worker in light and colors, from the very first I was always sure to leave myself an escape other than through art or death, I remain perfectly capable of stopping from one day, one hour, one minute to the next, and this is why I can continue doing what I do which is to work at art, persist in working with light and colors, so-called art has never seized me the way it has others, this take it or leave it attitude is what saves me in the end, life, yes, perhaps life itself the only legitimate escape, life the last best, the only hope for the final disappearance of the self, I need neither art nor death for that." We sat in silence for a spell.

It was a silence beyond the intermittent absences of sound in the cafeteria, a deeper, a more consuming silence which both reassured as well as confused me, the way my father's periodic silences both reassured as well as confused me.

On my birth my father had named me after himself.
Martin Blocker.
Not even the 'Junior' was ever allowed to be added after my name,
In time I saw this both as a curse as well as a blessing, for better or worse my father setting out to create me in his own image or at the very least to create someone to whom he could fearlessly and unreservedly reveal himself, I don't think he ever considered the burdens this placed on me, no, his only concern with having someone to whom he could shamelessly reveal himself, never mind that I turned out neither astute nor passionate enough to fulfill this role to any serious degree, my presence, my very existence sufficient for my father's needs.

After a prolonged and hopeless struggle my mother died shortly after having birthed me and this too my father took as a sign that I now belonged, existed only for him, that in time and with time I would come to not only appreciate but reflect his ways of thinking, his very life perhaps, become a so-called artist, a worker in art like himself, and in this he was only somewhat or mildly mistaken, because of my very obvious challenges, failures in all other spheres of life, only art remained for which I seemed to have a certain aptitude if no outstanding talent, his lengthy lectures aside we communicated through drawings and sketches, which suited both of us although at times less than others, we existed in a world of our own, that is his creation, and throughout my younger and even later years I could not nor did I want to conceive of another manner of making my way through life.

My father worked in spurts.

For long periods of time he would simply sit and stare at a blank canvas, I copied him in this as in everything else, in a different corner of our apartment, our so-called studio, I would sit and stare at my own blank canvas, we would both sit and stare as if waiting for something to occur within and without, my father rarely if ever made a distinction between the two, only my sitting and waiting entirely different from his I was quite convinced, his sitting and staring and waiting from a kind of effortless silence that I had to struggle for without ever finally attaining, my mind forever on the move that all my attempts to slow down only produced the opposite of their desired effect, my father as if lost to me then, inhabiting one world while I another, it was only when he finally started working that our worlds fused in a manner of speaking and I felt comfortable in imitating, copying the movements of his brush without of course ever achieving the same results he had.

"Everything about energy of course," he once told me. "The source of our so-called art as well as our very lives. And energy in quanta, read your books of physics, Martin, any so-called constant flow of energy is sheer sham, utter fakery, the second, the third, the fifth rate artists content to harness this fake, this deceptive flow, the true, the quantified energy escapes them in the end, they lack the patience, the power not to mention inspiration to become one with it, they are much too eager to assert without first negating, and it is only through negation that this true quantified energy can be recognized and made use of."

My father's so-called works of art, his productions in light and color capturing something beyond the reaches of time, first negating and then and only then asserting, I have witnessed patrons of his so-called art stand in front of one of his productions for hours at a time without later recalling why or for how long, like my father's so-called productions his patrons too seemed to have been caught outside of time without fully understanding and appreciating the mechanics involved.

Now and again my father made use of models, so-called models who came to our apartment, to our studio ostensibly to pose for him, all of them rather serious and attractive young women who in addition to making fairly good money felt they were somehow serving art, placing themselves at the service of a so-called great artist, nothing but nothing could have been further from the truth, my father simply appreciated their company, their presence in our so-called studio, "Nothing," he once confided to me, "there is nothing so solitary, so lonely as working at, trying to produce so-called works of art," he made sure to be moderately demanding in posing them now one way, now another but this was done simply for their own benefit and not his, he wanted them to feel that they were truly earning their money and not simply wasting their time, in the end he simply proceeded to paint, to work with his brushes in total disregard of the models, their very presence and subsequent denial of their presence all he was after, I can say for a fact that his finished works, his so-called productions of art had absolutely nothing to do with his models, bore not even the slightest resemblance to his models, he was careful to keep them in the dark, never ever to allow them even a single glimpse of what he was working at, and this is how he got his reputation, at least among his models, of being a rather eccentric, quirky artist, although they never actually complained, my father going out of his way to treat them like visiting royalty deigning to spend a few hours in his company.

"In the end," my father told me, "an artist, genuine artist cannot escape, turn his back on the solitary nature of his work, he may mitigate his surroundings, the very circumstances in which such solitary efforts must take place, make them more or less agreeable, it all depends, but sooner or later there comes a need, an absolute need to face only himself and then in facing himself even to surpass, to leave himself behind, and in this nothing and no one can help him, they can only hinder, fool himself into thinking that he is working at a so-called genuine work of art when all the time he is still trapped, caught in the world all around him from which he must absolutely free himself if he is to produce anything resembling a genuine work of art."

"You take someone like Van Gogh," my father told me, "who by the way was one of the few genuine artists, but standing in front of, no, confronted with one of his paintings, and the later the better, his wheat fields or starry nights or even his room at Arles, and you have to, you can't avoid asking yourself what this man, this artist was all about, in other words what his demands were on himself as well as on his viewers, and to my mind they were one and the same, the sharing of a vision so unequivocally intense as to leave no room for doubt or even any sort of thinking, in all but most especially in his later works someone like Van Gogh sails past all doubt and even thinking, doubt and even thinking the greatest enemies of so-called genuine art, art of the very first order, in the end it was Van Gogh's intense, genuine vision that sustained, kept him alive for as long as it had and his doubts and even thinking that drove him to his death, to his possible suicide, all but most especially his later works posing the most serious questions about life while answering them at the same time, in other words the questions become the very answers if the viewer knows how to see, how to enter them, his genuine works of art that is, and most don't, they are simply incapable or unwilling to leave themselves so open to such an experience, and while they become fully aware of the immense, even ridiculous demands of such works of art they simply content themselves with merely discussing and categorizing them, or if they possess obscene wealth of purchasing and owning them, as though anyone ever could own such genuine works of art, in other words they do their best to pull the genuine, the real into all the fakeries of this world, it is simply the way they deal with it much the way they deal with others and themselves, only fear and greed, and they are really inseparable, but only fear and greed are at the heart of their so-called art appreciation, but someone like Van Gogh forever escapes them and this is something they cannot abide, possibly put up

with, no, they won't be satisfied until they drag someone like Van Gogh
and his genuine works of art into this miserable world they all inhabit,
in other words they won't be satisfied until they have these true works
of art decorate the walls of their banks, their corporate headquarters or
worse, hanging on the walls of their living or bedrooms for their private
amusement, Van Gogh the man and the artist never truly penetrated
let alone understood, how could he be when these so-called art aficio-
nados are incapable of any real penetration let alone understanding of
themselves."

Difficult to interrupt, to stop my father once he got going in this
fashion. All my questions as if stillborn, locked within me, my father
could not, would not be disturbed to consider let alone to try to answer
them.

"An artist's," my father continued, "a so-called great artist's sole
concern is with time and distances, to escape the one and eliminate
the other, no artist worth his salt sets himself any other goal but this,
his very work goes to the very heart of these major problems of life,
and the two intricately, in fact causally bound, in other words if time
then distances and if distances then time, from his very first attempt to
create genuine art, a so-called great, a real artist sets out to surpass, to
negate both time and distances, embraces an all but impossible task at
which he is bound to fail in the end although his so-called failures are
so much more intense as well as communicative than anyone else's so-
called successes, but from the very first, are you listening, Martin, from
the very first his concern is with the impossible and never the possible,
other so-called second, third and fifth rate artists are perfectly content
at tackling only the possible at which they succeed, of course they do, to
their own and everyone else's satisfaction, but never, please listen, never
do they succeed in creating a real, a genuine, a lasting work of art, which
is basically an impossibility, because all of us, Martin, even so-called
great, genuine artists are made of nothing but time and distances, but
more than any others, more than anyone else they recognize this from
the start and set out to negate, to explode it, they more than anyone
else feel this trap of time and distances, this separation of themselves

from everyone and everything else around them, and this, the very real pain of this recognition initiates their journey to become one with everything they see and hear and smell and touch and feel, they are after the kind of unity, of oneness which is probably impossible to achieve through art and only temporarily, intermittently through some other way perhaps, but this doesn't keep them from trying, which is what after all makes them real, genuine and even so-called great artists, the fact that they never stop trying, they embrace their impossibilities the way others embrace their mediocrity, yes, they even embrace their so-called failures the way others embrace their so-called successes."

As he so often did with me, my father talked himself into a state of mental and physical exhaustion, he stared at me through vacant eyes as if failing to recognize his one and only true listener, he returned to his blank canvas then as I did to mine, "In the end we must negate all words and even art itself, Martin," he finally told me, "the art of negation the only true, the only legitimate art which in the end might yet enable us to see whatever is worth seeing."

"There are genre artists," my father told me, "thousands, hundreds of thousands of so-called genre artists, so-called landscape, abstract and human figure artists who set to produce, to give their viewers certain fragmented visions of life, mind you, never a whole, an entire vision of life but only certain fragmented visions of it, a truly whole and entire vision of life well beyond their capacities as well as passions, yes, in the end they give their viewers only what they truly deserve and are capable of digesting, so in a sense you can blame their viewers' tastes as much as you can these artists' limited passions and abilities, but faulting everyone is like faulting no one, no, the final and most serious blame rests with these so-called genre artists and no one else."

My head spinning at times.

Now and again a need, an irresistible urge to escape my father's words as well as his confining environment, at times I would disappear for hours, even days at a time knowing full well the dangers involved, an existence, yes, even a temporary existence on my own was more than

I could reasonably pull off, my so-called survival skills limited to my close and ongoing contact with my father, but I would wander the city then without caring where I was headed or what I would do once I got there, in the end the only problem that remained was finding my way back home to my father's nurturing but also constricting world, for the longest time it was the only one I could exist and properly function in, "Are you all right?" my father would simply ask on my return without pressing for details on my prior doings and whereabouts, by neither action nor word did he ever betray a single sign of agitation at my temporary absences, "Of course, Martin," he would tell me, "of course one day you'll leave for good, you'll leave without bothering to return, but that day still far off as you and I both realize, you've still so much to learn and what you need to learn you can only learn from me, you're not yet in a position of teaching yourself, but one day, Martin, one day for sure, teacher and taught will exist as one in no one but yourself."

I nodded.

What else could I do under the circumstances?

For better or worse my father's hold on me much too strong to combat at the time, and even if it hadn't been I lacked both the desire as well as the power of will to finally and definitively sever my ties with the man.

Now and again my father spoke of moving to the country, entertained the notion in a most wistful, romantic and therefore highly unrealistic fashion, a move to his so-called dacha in the country which from the pictures he had shown me was nothing more than a rundown, defunct farmhouse, it may well have been a working farm once, but, no, no longer, certainly not by the time he had purchased it years ago, the untended fields, the rotting structure and no doubt the varieties of animals seeking refuge there, "For a few years your mother and I extremely happy there," he once confided, but as he kept from going into any details I could hardly credit the veracity of his statement, was he already a so-called great artist then or simply a frustrated man contemplating, hoping to become one, no, I could not envision any sort of real happiness for my mother in the company of such a man, such a would-be artist, yes, no doubt he drove her crazy with his words as well as his silences the way he occasionally did me, and this without even his art as a point of fusion and balance, and the surrounding country itself with its morose predictabilities and repetitive cycles must have driven her crazy as well, from the few remaining photographs of my mother she did not at all strike me as a so-called country person but much more a city dweller type, her face, her smile, her very bearing and even her clothes those of a city dweller and not at all of a so-called country person, yes, something at once genteel and sophisticated about her entire appearance, no doubt my father had dragged her to the country much against her will where he could set about molding and possibly destroying her much the way he so often attempted to mold and destroy me as well, and this all the while he was molding and destroying himself at the same time, in other words destroying the man he had been and molding the so-called great, so-called significant artist he thought he was destined to become, but this did not keep him from occasionally musing about a return to this dilapidated, miserable farmhouse, this so-called dacha where it no doubt all began and would possibly end, ,but his musings of a highly romantic and therefore ridiculous nature as I already indicated.

"Listen, listen to me, Martin. It's only in the country that a man, an artist can come face to face with himself, truly face himself, in time and through time in the city he finds himself challenged on all sides, his ideas, his very being challenged on all sides, the city with its myriad reflections never truly reflects the real man, the genuine artist, the city with a way of reflecting nothing but itself, its mediocre and therefore totally useless and even destructive reflections, even its so-called source of inspiration is always a negative and never a positive one, an artist, a real, a genuine artist if he persists, for whatever reason, in working in the city does so in an entirely negative and never a positive fashion, in other words in producing his so-called works of art he has first to tackle, to eliminate the city's myriad negative influences, the city's sole concern only with itself and never with the individual or the individual's so-called artistic struggles, the city's reaction to a so-called genuine work of art is to subsume, to incorporate it into itself and so destroy every ounce of individuality that work may possess, the city absolutely uncaring and destructive in this regard, it may pride itself on occasionally recognizing talent but never the real, the unique in any particular work of art which it quite rightly regards as a challenge to its very existence, the city's main concern is always with the business of art and never its true, its essential nature, real comprehension beyond its limited capabilities, any hint of real comprehension would threaten its fake solidity, smash it to smithereens, the city's sole business is buying and selling, it wants to have nothing to do with what it can neither buy nor sell, and this may be all right, even attractive at the start of an artist's, yes, even a genuine artist's career, an artist setting out to make a so-called name for himself, but not later, no, not when neither his name nor his so-called lucrative sales matter to the genuine artist, in every fiber of his being then he finds the city's oppressive forces allied against him, no, the city will not rest until it makes the real, the genuine artist into its puppet like all the thousands of mediocre artists attempting to make a living there, all of them mere replicates, duplicates of one another whose main concern is survival and not the production of true works of art, all artists sign a so-called spiritual contract with the city through which they surrender their individuality to the city's mass interests, nothing, then, nothing remains for the real, the genuine artist but to turn his back on, to move as far away from the city as he possibly can, to move deep into the country where nature neither accepts nor rejects his so-called works of art, where it imposes neither strictures nor any sort of negative or even positive judgments, in other words where the genuine artist is left entirely free to produce whatever he will while depending on no one's approval or condemnation other than his own."

My father's occasional outbursts, his vicious attacks on the city and lavish praise of the country lasting for longer or shorter periods depending on his moods, but through his subsequent actions or rather inactions it became clear to me that he was in no way ready to desert the one and embrace the other, they were simply his way of clearing the air, of ridding himself of his varieties of fears and hopes, "Never forget,

Martin," he once told me, "that a real, a genuine artist must be both fearless and hopeless," and then he, I, we simply returned to business as usual, my father little caring about the effects of his tirades on me, of leaving me at sea regarding his true feelings, no, so long as he cleared the air, got his confusions out of his system things went on as before with only I somewhat or even quite a bit worse for the wear.

Our apartment, our studio decorated with works of so-called primitive art from different places and periods. Paintings, masks, statuettes, even some weaponry that seemed to speak to my father in a most direct and unobstructed fashion that few works of so-called western art ever did.

In between his so-called productions, his ongoing attempts at working with light and colors he would sit and contemplate these to me, alien works from other places and periods, my father then as if addressing his words directly to these alien works as well as to himself with I myself simply overhearing, legitimizing his speaking out loud with no other listeners present.

"This is art with a small not a capital A, all art with a capital A nothing but exalted fakeries, this is the only true, the only legitimate art with these artists fully at one with their societies, their environments, there is no need for them to expand, to waste their energies on denying and negating their societies and environments, they are completely free to focus all their energies, their so-called artistic energies on expressing the very lives of their societies, their environments, of becoming entirely one with them. Imagine a modern, a so-called western artist attempting to do the same. He would either succeed in producing the most mediocre, infantile and therefore insulting works of art, as so many, most of our so-called artists actually do, or drive himself crazy, stark raving mad in the process, no, in order to create a so-called genuine work of art our modern, our western artists have to first negate, destroy everything about their societies' numbing and pernicious influence, and then perhaps create or recreate them in ways they had never existed before, yes, the only hope for our modern, our western artists lies not in fusion but separation, not in a fusion with the outward trappings, the fake values of their societies but in a complete denial and separation from them, in other words our true, our genuine modern artist has no choice but to exist and work entirely on his own, that is in and for himself, and this was definitely and most obviously not the case with these so-called primitive artists, who drew their very strength and sources of inspiration from their environments and societies, and who in this way produced a certain type of real, of genuine art which our modern artists are capable of producing only through denials and the kind of solitary existence these so-called primitive artists could never have imagined."

After these musings, meditations of his on primitive artists my father often with a need to escape their visceral influence, incongruously he went for long walks in the city which he had just ranted and raved against, he dragged me along if only to provide himself with a pretend audience in case his musings, his meditations should once more assert themselves.

"The tension that exists in the modern artist, and I'm only talking of the real, the genuine artist, between his outer and inner visions is something totally alien to the real, the genuine primitive artist, the modern artist's innate mistrust of what's too readily apparent never manifested in the primitive one, outer and inner visions one and the same for the so-called primitive artist where they must not, cannot be the same for the genuine so-called modern artist, the so-called modern, western artist has nothing to gain and everything to lose from his outward visions, and conversely he has everything to gain and nothing to lose from his inner ones, he must completely mistrust the former and absolutely trust the latter, as a matter of fact there is a nearly irrepressible longing in the so-called modern, western artist to return to, to become a so-called primitive one, yes, just look at the productions of certain fertile periods of serious artists like Picasso, Matisse and a few others besides, during those periods they toyed, experimented with returning to or actually becoming primitive artists, none of this worked in the long run of course, for a so-called modern, a western artist can in no way become a so-called primitive one, he can no more embrace a mythical past than he can turn his back on the substantive present, and this no matter how inviting the one and repulsive the other, no, he must find a new, his own peculiar way of sailing beyond them both, of measuring himself by no one's standards but his own, even though such measurements are practically impossible since both the measurements as well as the measurer are one and the same, still, what other choice does he have if he means to avoid becoming a second, a third or a fifth rate artist who endlessly continues duplicating others as well as himself, who in the process becomes not just a second-hand artist but a second-hand human being as well."

On these long walks with my father I often lagged behind, my father slowing down then speeding up in a most unpredictable fashion, yes, almost as though his walks were intended to complement, to keep pace with his ever changing thoughts, and then after awhile I experienced an almost physical, a visceral fear of becoming crushed by the crowds below and the immense buildings above, lacking my father's powerful inner world my means of combating this fear extremely limited, space and time collided in my head to the point of nearly annihilating me, I was yet nowhere near creating my own space and time the way my father often told me a genuine artist absolutely needed to, my acts of negation only weakly manifested and those of assertion not yet in evidence, on more than one occasion I returned enervated and exhausted from these walks, quite the opposite of my father who returned energized and ready to work after these so-called confrontations with the city, he attacked his canvas with a renewed vigor and inspiration whereas I sat immobile in front of mine, regarding my own blank canvas as though I were staring into the vast emptiness of my very soul.

My father rarely sought out the company of other artists, he regarded nearly all forms of socializing as a waste on his part and little more than insults on theirs, "All artists the same," he confided to me, "their feigned interest in others' works nothing more than veiled, hypocritical attempts to turn the focus, the spotlight onto themselves, their sole topic, their main concern is only with themselves, they will play their hypocritical games only so long as necessary to clear the ground as it were, only until they feel it's safe to begin talking about themselves, to start expounding their half-baked, their inane theories about art in general and their own in particular, they use terms like 'expression' and 'strength' and 'meaning' when they have no, no, absolutely no idea of what those terms were ever intended to signify, they are filled with theories and ideas without ever suspecting that neither theories nor ideas have anything to do with real, with genuine art, their conversations empty, substance less, as shabby in other words as is their general physical appearance, they pretend to reach for the moon, the stars when all they're doing is digging deep holes in which to bury their pitiful selves, and once started they won't stop until they feel they will have explained their art, themselves to everyone's full satisfaction including their own, most especially their own, little realizing that explanations are anathema to true, genuine art as well as to true, genuine human beings, that real, genuine art exists in and for itself the way true, genuine human beings exist strictly in and for themselves, that any and all explanations are not only insufficient but become real stumbling blocks to any true appreciation of so-called genuine art as well as genuine human beings."

In spite of his very real aversion to the company of fellow artists, my father frequently organized so-called artistic evenings where everyone was warned in advance that there were to be no, absolutely no artistic discussions, although this dictum of his disregarded almost from the very first arrival of his very first guests, in other words his so-called guests, his fellow artists making little or no effort to leave their so-called artistic worlds behind in order to embrace and discuss the world of social, political and economic events which my father occasionally longed to do, but my father fully suspected and even knew that in no time after their arrival his so-called fellow artists would begin to shamelessly exhibit and explore their own artistic worlds and this in a most subjective and therefore annoying and even meaningless fashion, that his social gatherings, his so-called artistic evenings would soon enough turn into playful but at times vicious duels concerning the merits of one artistic world opposed to others, that these guests of his came equipped with nothing but ideas of their own merits, their so-called artistic selves in mind, that they were ready to do battle to both reveal and defend them, that everything they saw and felt and thought they saw and felt and thought through the confining and therefore distorting lens of the very center of their artistic worlds, their artistic selves, that in the end they would have nothing, no, absolutely nothing to say, to contribute about the world at large, nothing, that is, in the way of any thoughtful or even mildly interesting analysis, my father put up with this for as long as he could, tried to keep himself in the background and simply watch, observe without bothering to listen, at one level he felt he could and in fact did for awhile enjoy these fellow artists of his as simple human beings with their all too human faults and misconceptions, their so-called artistic misconceptions, but in spite of the numbing, the mellowing effects of alcohol, at some point in the evening, and at times the least expected, the most inconvenient point he felt he had no choice but to call it quits, to announce in a most firm and even dictatorial fashion that the so-called artistic evening was now at an end, that they should all gather themselves up and leave his apartment, his studio without another thing thought or said, that he was extremely sorry but this combination of his migraine headache, and company was more than he could handle, that he now needed absolute quiet and solitary darkness to keep from going stark raving mad, in other words at the sudden end of these artistic evenings he nearly always managed to offend every last one of his guests, his so-called fellow artists who grumbled and swore that never ever would they attend one of his social gatherings, his so-called artistic evenings, and this in spite of the outstanding food and booze he had ordered from the city's finest delicatessen and the most exclusive liquor store, and my father swore and grumbled as well that never again would he invite his fellow artists, his so-called guests to one of his evening gatherings, that his social, his so-called artistic evening were now definitely at an end, they weren't of course, in spite of the insults traded and swallowed he would time and again invite them and they time again show up at our door only to have these gatherings, these artistic evenings end in the same insults and fiasco, these scenes endlessly repeated with neither my father nor his so-called guests learning from their mistakes of the past.

His eyes shut, my father collapsed in his easy-chair.

"Do you believe, Martin," he mumbled, "did you see, hear, witness what went on? Like a bunch of jackals sniffing, whining, barking, they came ready for the kill, the carcasses of other egos as well as their own, they would not stop until they devoured and digested everything in sight including themselves, the stench of their so-called artistic ideas filling every square inch of this apartment, seeping into the furniture and even the very walls, we'll have to air this place for days to get rid of it, working in the crisp, the bitter cold a small price to pay as far as I'm concerned, never, do you hear me, Martin, never will I put myself, put you through this again, I would rather have myself devoured by inane critics than have to listen to the vain and empty ideas of fellow artists, to have their hand-me-down ideas invade my very soul, I have absolutely nothing in common with these people and they nothing in common with me, that we're all so-called artists is a sheer accident of nature and has nothing, no, absolutely nothing to do with who and what we are, I would rather spend time with bus conductors, doormen and street sweepers than these so-called fellow artists, there is nothing, no, absolutely nothing to be learned from fellow artists while there might, in fact I'm sure there are any number of things to be learned from bus conductors, doormen and street sweepers, an important lesson for you, Martin, never waste your time with people who assert or pretend to know but only with those who readily confess they don't, if you are to become a real, a genuine artist, Martin, you must run from fellow artists as if from the very fires of hell and embrace the coarse, the common, the so-called insignificant people all around, who as a matter of fact are neither coarse nor common although, yes, insignificant, most certainly insignificant in the eyes of the world, but in the last, the final analysis it's only the insignificant that count, everything that can be learned can

only be learned from them, Martin, yes, you must embrace the insignificant and avoid the significant at all costs if you are ever to become a real
artist, a genuine human being."

As much as he ranted and raved against museums my father could
hardly avoid constantly visiting them, steadfastly dragging me along in
the pursuit of so-called mental anguish as well as unalloyed pleasure.
Not even inclement weather allowed to interfere, in fact the worse the
weather, rain, sleet, snow, what have you, the more he insisted on our
setting out and visiting one or another of them.

"Museums pretend to be worlds within the world," he told me,
"havens as well as so-called repositories of our so-called cultural past,
in truth they merely sap your physical and creative energies to leave you
confused, exhausted and spent in the end, seeing too much is worse
than seeing nothing at all, in fact like certain cheap restaurants with
their all-that-you-can-eat buffets museums pride themselves on serving
up enormous portions and varieties of food with little or no regard to
either quality or style of presentation, their main goal is to encourage
their customers to simply gorge themselves, to stuff their faces, their
bellies, their minds to bursting, to devour everything in sight without
properly digesting a single significant item, museums will not rest until
everyone has eaten to the point of nausea and exhaustion, like everyone
else, 'the more the merrier' is their single motto, something like 'the less
the better' simply scares them to death, everyone who enters a museum
must do so at his own considerable risk, head for just a handful or even
one or two significant works of art and spend some solitary, quality
time with those while disregarding all the rest, do you understand what
I'm telling you, Martin, we must enter the doors of a museum like
entering a prison, a trap while always remembering, keeping in mind
the way back out, the route of escape to keep from becoming perpetual
prisoners, all the doors to all the museums nothing but trap doors which
we must recognize as soon as we enter them, yes, because only with this
wariness, this alert attitude will we have a fighting chance of emerging
sane and whole at the end of our visit."

We paused in front of a work by Klee, in front of several works by Klee.

"Look, Martin, look. Please, just sit still and look.

"Unlike Van Gogh who was a great artist because of a driving passion that he had no choice but to communicate, Klee was a great one, although perhaps not as great, but still a so-called great artist because of the clarity as well as simplicity of his vision, a supreme reductionist in fusing both his inner and outer worlds, in viewing his works one cannot escape the feeling that from the first, yes, perhaps from the very first, first he knew just what he was after, this clarity, this simplicity in fusing the inner and outer worlds, the mythological as well as the real, in his works the mythical becomes reality and reality the mythical, do you see this, Martin, in other words even if the worlds he creates don't actually exist they are just as real within their own boundaries as anything we see around us, and all this reduced to simple lines, shapes and vibrant, even outlandish colors, yes, Klee was a great artist not because he was overwhelmed by the world like Van Gogh but because he stepped back and viewed it as well as himself with mythical scholarly or scholarly mythical eyes, yes, let's just remain here for awhile and come to terms with Klee's simplicity and clarity, tackle Klee's simplicity and clarity today and nothing else, that'll be enough and even more than enough for today I think, yes, I have no wish to go wandering about this tomb of a museum, Klee is enough for now, we'll just stay here until we will have come to terms with, fully digested his vision."

On our way back home the driving rain a decided advantage.

It embraced us even as we embraced it in a purely physical and non-intellectual fashion, it freed us of the museum's and, yes, even of Klee's hold on us, my father leading the way in his customary fashion and I following in mine, both of us soaked to the skin by the time we arrived at the refuge of our apartment, our so-called studio.

My father speaking of dreamscapes of the country.

"No, certainly not your unusual, your creative dreams, as a young man I was not yet capable of dreaming those, these were dreamscapes of an entirely different, a negative sort, the very monotony and drabness of the country what I needed at the time, I could easily have picked a better, a far lovelier spot to settle in, surround myself with nature's so-called unending and ever changing beauty, immerse myself and in time and with time become a so-called painter of such beauty, a so-called landscape artist of the third, second and perhaps even of the first order, but that's just what I didn't want, I instinctively knew I wanted to become a somewhat or even altogether different artist, in other words my move to the country intended as a cure for the facile, the infectious beauty of the country, the destructive because all too readily available beauty of the country, that's why I bought this ridiculous farmhouse situated in the most drab and despicable part of the country, dragged your poor mother to this gray, this brown, this grayish brown part of the country, your poor mother who was as close to being a saint as I ever hope to meet, a saint at least as far as I was concerned, who at the time would have followed me to the ends of the earth if I had asked her to, who at the time had no, absolutely no idea of my ulterior motive in moving to this awful part of the country, yes, in retrospect but perhaps even at the time I judged myself guilty of having dragged her away from her familiar surroundings only to be driven crazy and eventually killed by the very monotony and drabness of this so-called country, but that's what true, genuine artists or even those who have a notion of becoming true, genuine artists do, you see, sooner or later they manage to drive crazy or even eventually kill everyone they hold near and dear, everyone who loves them in some fashion or other, no, in the process of negating everything for their art's sake they won't rest until they negate everyone near and dear to them as well, kill off everyone near and dear to them and while it's true that the immediate causes of your mother's death were the complications after your birth, the secondary, the indirect and therefore more sinister cause was my dragging her to this mind numbing part of the country, and all this for nothing more than art, even if it is so-called true, genuine art, never mind, but after several years of living, existing in this most destructive part of the country I did indeed see the light or experienced a shock of realization of what was and wasn't true beauty, of what did and didn't constitute genuine art, that true beauty as well as true art were to be found, to be birthed from within and not without, yes, at least as far as I was concerned, and it was then and only then I began my most serious and all-consuming work in light and colors, yes, after that shock there was no more question in my mind that my only worthwhile work would always be in and with light and colors, and then and only then the move back to the city which was by then no longer necessary for the development of my art just as the mind numbing country was no longer necessary for the development of my art, although the city, yes, the city absolutely necessary for the development of my so-called career, my flourishing as a real, a genuine artist, which over the years I've come to increasingly regret of course, this whole notion of a career, of flourishing as a real, a genuine artist nothing but a sham, a mask, a detriment to the very art it was originally intended to support, in fact in time and with time the city as destructive to true, genuine art as the mind numbing country, even more so, and this in spite of the city's offering certain so-called cultural advantages never ever to be found in the country, and it's only for the sake of these so-called cultural advantages that one puts up with all the dirt, noise and general madness of the city which is entirely different from the madness of the country, but for how long, Martin, yes, that's the question, for how long, no doubt there will come a time when we will have no choice but to trade one madness for the other, I just want you to be prepared, and that too for the sake of so-called true, so-called genuine art or perhaps for something else, something entirely different of which as yet I have absolutely no idea, but it will happen one day, of this I'm sure, and I just want you to be prepared."

My father unquestionably a gifted artist, an artist of the first rank but basically an extremely selfish, self-involved human being.

And I just the opposite.

An artist of limited, of questionable gifts but for better or worse a nearly selfless, an almost entirely ambitionless human being.

Which is why I suspect we got along as well as we have for all these years, my father seeing himself reflected in my eyes and I merely hoping to see myself reflected in his, and it's the same even now in my recollection, my father, although long dead, still seeing himself reflected in my eyes and I still hoping to see myself reflected in his,, we could have hardly borne each other's company if that had not been the case, that is if my father had ceased seeing his own reflection in my eyes and I hoping to see mine in his, failing this we would have bored each other to death or worse, outright killed each other, in other words disappeared from each other's lives because of this ongoing clash of differences in our very natures, but because my father never surrendered the hope of making me into his likeness and I never ceased hoping of becoming his true reflection we stayed with each other for as long as we did, until his actual, his physical death in fact, no, I know of no other instance of father and son, of so-called artistic fathers and sons remaining with one another, leading parallel lives in the closest of proximities until the actual demise, the irrevocable disappearance of one of them, and this in spite of all the sane, rational, in fact logical reasons mitigating against it, all the first but even the second or fifth rate artists I can think of managed at some point of their lives, their so-called artistic lives to break the hold of, to sever their ties with their so-called father teachers or teacher fathers, and I'm thinking of your Picassos, your Dürers and even of your Cellinis, Cimabues, what have you, no, at some point of their lives, their so-called artistic lives they simply had to break the hold of, sever their links to their teaching fathers or father teachers to strike out on their own, to begin to discover things on their own, and perhaps, although by now it's difficult if not impossible to assert, but perhaps this was the very thing my father wanted for me all along, something I should have but completely failed to recognize, no, something definitely lacking, missing in my so-called artistic makeup, an absence of intensity, passion and will to assert myself as even a fledgling artist in my own right, and not just an artist, no, but a fledgling human being as well, the truth of the matter was that in all my years with my father I was never malcontent enough with his company to sever my binding and at times numbing ties to him, nor he with mine to sever his, it took his death, his actual demise to bring this about, in other words an irrevocable act of fatality and fate to accomplish this, in other words given my father with his very real and genuine artistic personality and given me with a nearly total absence of the same it was inevitable that we should be bound, linked together until his death, no, neither of us in a position to change this absolute, this given, no, neither of us capable of changing our lives in any positive or even negative fashion, both of us as if stuck in a groove from the moment we first laid eyes on each other, from the moment I exited my mother's womb only to be firmly seized and held in my father's arms.

"All art," my father said, "all so-called real and genuine art nothing, nothing but child's play. Even Picasso, yes, the truest and most genuine artist I know, although he had quite a bit of the poseur, the salesman in him, too much perhaps, no matter, but even someone like Picasso said as much, once unashamedly admitting that all his life, his so-called artistic life he had been trying to learn or relearn to paint like a child, of course by then he was Picasso the real, the genuine artist and would and did paint like a child as Picasso the genuine artist, but my point still valid I think, every so-called true and genuine art is something of an attempted return to the truest and most genuine art of children, of some children at any rate, and most real, genuine artists forget or never directly face this, yes, even so-called true, genuine artists opt for the complicated over the simple, the adulterated over the pure, they continually stumble over themselves in their efforts to create so-called great, meaningful and lasting art, in other words at some point in their careers they begin to take themselves most seriously, begin to substitute their so-called artistic worlds for the world all around them, little realizing that in the last and even in the first analysis it's life, the world all around them that truly matters and not any so-called artistic world, no matter how genuine, how real, and it's this seriousness, are you listening, Martin, but this seriousness of great, of genuine artists that becomes their undoing in the end, the very death of their so-called artistic worlds as well as the world all around them, it's their very seriousness that makes them run smack into and do battle with themselves, a losing battle I might add, for how could it be otherwise, yes, very few true, genuine artists survive unscathed, avoid killing off their so-called genuine art as well as themselves, life, you see, the marvelous chaos, the glorious messiness of life gets them all in the end, because that, you see, are you listening, Martin, that is not something even the best of so-called real, so-called genuine art can ever hope to capture let alone pit itself against, I just hope I'm making myself clear, somewhat clear at any rate, and I think I knew or at any rate suspected this from the start, yes, from my very first recognition, my shock of realization of what it might mean to be a true, a genuine artist, I think I knew or at any rate suspected, that with this initial recognition or realization would come the eventual seriousness, the most abhorrent and self-destructive seriousness that only a handful of artists have ever managed to survive, which is why from the very first I worked only in light and colors and continued ever after to work in nothing but light and colors, which is not to say I've succeeded, succeeded in my so-called art perhaps but not in entirely, fully avoiding this disease of seriousness, this lethal and most artistic disease of seriousness, to this day I fear and remain constantly on guard against this most lethal and artistic disease, and who knows but in the end this may not be enough, all my cautions and precautions may not suffice to save me, to save me from myself, you see, but don't look so confused, now and again you have a most annoying way of looking confused, I simply wanted you to know what I'm thinking, what's going through my mind, things will no doubt be somewhat or even entirely different with you, so, spare me your looks of confusion, nothing more detrimental to an artist than confusion of any sort, for better or worse he must create from an absolute certainty no matter what, yes, even at the price of his art's, his own destruction at the end."

Silence overwhelmed us both.

"A deafening silence," as my father so often put it.

Without moving he stood in front of his blank canvas for the longest time, and as in other things I copied him in this as well, without moving I stood in front of my blank canvas for the longest while, and now, I thought, now we will never work again, never pick up our brushes and work again, my father in his light and colors and I in my ridiculous, my pathetic imitation of them, but, no, the passage of time not withstanding my father once more picked up his brush and began to work and I followed suit, and in this fashion we somehow managed to push ourselves beyond my father's condemning words, if that's what they were, and we worked late into the evening without another word passing between us.

"Art," my father was saying, "all genuine, all real art is nothing but a struggle against the ordinary, the routine. The ordinary, the routine forever in danger of capturing us, of holding us captive, for ransom as it were, there is nothing, trust me, Martin, nothing worse than being caught, trapped by the ordinary, the routine, it's the death of art, the very spirit of art and all so-called creativity, take my word for it, that's why all artists, so-called great, genuine artists do their utmost to struggle against the ordinary, the routine, of course the danger, the ever present danger here is that their very struggles become ordinary, routine, that is in time and with time I'm talking about, that their very search for the extraordinary in the ordinary becomes just an ordinary, a routine search, yes, in fact all their avoidance to keep it from becoming ordinary and routine becoming routine and ordinary as well, yes, pay attention, Martin, there remains little or nothing to be done, in the end I'm talking of, but this little or nothing, yes, nothing, may yet become a salvation of sorts, a salvation for both the artist and his art, you see, by doing nothing, by simply keeping still and doing absolutely nothing something may yet come to him, something fresh and new that had all but deserted him, that he had all but given up on, something seizing his mind, his brush, his very soul, I'm speaking metaphorically, and this after he had given up, totally surrendered to the routine, the ordinary, in other words his very mediocrity, seen right through although not beyond, no, certainly not beyond, and then, yes, only then something may yet happen, something firsthand and even breathtaking, and this not because of anything he does but because of what he doesn't do, yes, the saving grace, the salutary charm of nothingness, it may yet become the very sparkplug of creativity, I just hope you realize, have some inkling of what I'm talking about."

My father stared at his blank canvas.

These periods of his stillness, of his so-called inactivity grew progressively longer with the passage of time, they left me little to copy, to imitate, I tried working on my own with absolutely no reference or connection to his projects of the past, the results satisfying neither myself nor him, I could tell by the looks on his face, and while my father never actually criticized any of my works, certain looks of his more than sufficient to tell me just what he thought of them, all the same I went on working while he remained absolutely still, I had no choice I felt, my choices extremely limited at the time.

"You must see life as if in a flash," my father was saying, "truth, god help us, as if in a flash. In other words all at once or not at all."

Some of my father's most interesting, most incisive ideas came to him on our walks through the city park, when he appeared to desert, to turn his back on being a so-called real, a genuine artist, although he never completely did, no, I don't think so, my father no doubt finding it impossible to completely turn his back on, to irrevocably walk away from being a so-called true, a genuine artist.

The trees all bare. The smell and feel of winter all around us.

"The problem of course," he continued, "is to be able to let go. To recognize, no, to experience, no, to feel the flash and then let go. Not to try to seize, to capture, to cling to it in any fashion. Does this make any sense to you, Martin?"

A few strays following us.

Desiccated, miserable creatures with vacant yet searching eyes.

My father stopped to look at them, studying them with his usual intensity.

"And something else as well, Martin," he said, "something beyond this flash I mean. A real, a genuine artist must learn not to separate, to distinguish, to see the beautiful in the ugly and the ugly in the beautiful, in other words not to escape into ideas, the ideal, all such escapes useless, detrimental in the end, no, a true, a genuine artist must see the world exactly as it is, in and for itself I mean, the beautiful as well as the ugly, the so-called good as well as the so-called evil, and without this in any way confusing or even affecting him, and then, listen up, Martin, he must then see some sort of beauty in all this, although don't ask me how, this is neither the time nor the place, but some sort of beauty that will make him pick up his brush and paint in a way no one has ever painted before."

My father stared at the dogs without moving.

In other words he kept his distance even as the dogs kept theirs.

Yes.

My father then content with nothing but observation, a genuine although distant observation, it would have been much simpler and certainly more helpful to have called to the dogs and approached them in some way with the intention of taking them to a shelter or even to our home, our studio, but, no, such an idea would never have occurred to my father, the real, the genuine artist, as a real, a genuine artist my father perfectly content to merely observe and study without the need to act, to in any way insert himself into the world, and I both hated and loved him for this at the time, just as I still love and hate him after all these years, long after his demise when he is no more than just a character in my imagination.

From my earliest childhood I viewed my father as a problem to be solved. I promised myself no rest until I would solve this so-called problem of my father, and this without in any way understanding just what it was I was promising myself.

"A true artist won't stop," my father was saying, "until he will have seized and turned himself into his art, seized the entire world in fact and turned it into his art. And this is something instinctive, guttural, in other words beyond the mind and its multiple, endless ways of creating and then attempting to solve problems. Trouble is that artists, even your great, your genuine artists are still human beings, remain human beings no matter what, and as human beings they cannot shake their habits of approaching life as well as their art as problems to be solved, no, they simply fail or refuse to recognize that there are no real problems in either life or art that the mind hasn't first created then subsequently failed to solve, in the end they, like everyone else, drive themselves crazy in trying to solve these fake, these pseudo-problems that they themselves have created, that is, their minds have created, in their art as well as in their lives they set out to accomplish at once too much and not enough, the wrong sort of accomplishment, you see, and no matter how great and even meaningful these so-called genuine artists, most if not all remain nothing but so-called problem solvers to the very end, attempting to the very end to solve problems that they themselves have created, in other words problems that never have, do or will exist except for the interfering minds of artists as humans or humans as artists, and this is why from the very first I approached my so-called art in an entirely different fashion, knew from the very first that my art would neither create nor solve any problems, that I would be anything but a problem solving artist, which is why from the very first I started to work in nothing but light and colors, focused all my so-called artistic energies on nothing but light and colors, yes, from the very first I refused to recognize the so-called problem of art as well as that of life, I entertained few if any expectations, I saw both art and life in the simplest possible fashion, in other words for no more or less than what they actually were without my judgments, fears and hopes allowed to interfere, yes, from that flash or shock of insight I set out to accomplish nothing, do you understand, Martin, nothing but to work in light and colors, the only thing I realized is that I had no choice, I simply had to work in light and colors, and in retrospect this may have been a good thing or bad, I leave this to others, I'm incapable of making such judgments about myself, but the thing is I'm no longer sure, I don't mind confessing, Martin, whether my so-called art and entire life has been good or bad or even worse, simply inconsequential and therefore utterly meaningless."

Yes.

My father a problem to be solved.

Still, now, after all these years my father remaining a problem to be solved.

Curious.

My father, a true, a genuine artist although hardly ever what I would call a true, a genuine human being, no matter, but my father forever donning different masks, different human masks to suit the occasion, no, not artistic masks or mask, his so-called artistic mask always steadfast, always the same, but his human masks as varied as the occasions eliciting them, my father's ridiculous and unfailingly failed attempts to be all things to all people, and this strictly as a so-called pretend human being I'm talking about, no, not as an artist, as an artist he was entirely solitary, satisfied in standing completely alone, but as a so-called fake human being or any number of fake human beings he went to great lengths to convince the world that he was anything but that; but those, that as a fake human being he was at least as real, as genuine as all the so-called real human beings he ever encountered, that's why his occasionally curious mannerisms as well as his outlandish attires, his top hat, his cane and all the rest, my father's inevitable although consciously failed attempts to blend in as it were, to blend in that is as a human artist or an artistic human, and more, yes, perhaps there may have been something even more to this than that, in donning his varied and various human masks my father was also reflecting the varied and various human masks of others, showing how difficult if not impossible it was to be a real, a genuine human being, while it was less hard although equally impossible to be a real, a genuine artist, yes, but the more I analyze his actions, his behaviors as well as his so-called real, genuine art the more confused I become, once more or still I'm back with my father on one of our lengthy walks through that forested city park where I'm aware of the so-called forest all around while failing to distinguish, to recognize any individual tree, yes, and once more or still my father's words wash over me as if in a torrent where a mere trickle would have been much easier to digest, to comprehend, but in spite of all these difficulties I haven't given up, no, not yet, I have all the time in the world now and I haven't given up.

Yes.

My father a problem to be solved all right.

Is he still and was he ever?

No.

I'm not sure of even that any more.

"Running out of time," my father was saying. "You see how that works, Martin? First trapped in time then running out of it."

We were sitting in our apartment, our studio of multilayered light and colors, light and darkness. Surrounded by our visions, our genuine works of art, his at any rate, as well as by the very real and true works of so-called primitive art which now quietly, now loudly collided with those of our own.

"We are made of time stuff, Martin, never forget, everything we think and feel and accomplish nothing but time stuff, yes, in fact everything we see and smell and hear and touch nothing but time stuff as well, we are born into time and then die to it, step out of it as it were, yet all the while we're here, and it's the real, the genuine artist I'm talking of, we do, we attempt our best to move beyond, our very best efforts nothing but attempts to move beyond, don't nod, Martin, just listen, it's most annoying when you nod without actually listening."

Once again my father off and running.

Substituting words for his actual works of art, even though he mistrusted and even detested words as much as I did and still do.

"From the very first we are trapped and become increasingly entangled in time. All our ideas, our work, even our so-called genuine works of art accomplished in and through time, yes, even because of it, and I just hope you see the contradiction, the impossibility embedded in this, using time in our misguided attempts to move beyond time itself, which all so-called true, so-called genuine artists desire more than anything else, no, none of them, none of us will be satisfied until we will have conquered time in some fashion by somehow moving beyond it, and this even though we haven't a clue, no, not a single clue of what that might mean, and this because time is all we have and are, the only thing for us to work with, but how to go on experimenting, attempting, working in and through time except by fooling ourselves that at some point, yes, even now we might be moving beyond it, beyond time itself I'm talking about, you see the naked reality, Martin, the annoying impossibility, yes, I'm sure you do, yes, all of us, and this includes your great, your so-called genuine artists, perhaps even especially your true artists, but all of us doomed to remain forever trapped within the boundaries of time, they are the most powerful and pernicious boundaries I know, and no art, no matter how great, will ever break through it, but as artists, stop fidgeting, Martin, as true, as genuine artists what other choice is there, what other choice do we have than to consistently, persistently attempt that which can never be achieved, yes, we are like creatures forever approaching a wall, banging our heads against the wall until they're bloodied, look at me, Martin, pausing then, stepping back perhaps, only to return and get our heads bloodied once more," at the time I had no idea my father was quoting Wittgenstein, my father rarely if ever crediting so-called thinkers but only his true, his precious genuine artists, "yes, there is absolutely no hope for serious artists, and still they persist in a now hopeful but for the most part hopeless fashion, I want you to think about this, Martin, yes, as a would-be genuine artist you must think about and somehow come to terms with the nagging, the impossible questions raised by time, as a matter of fact in your thinking about it, it might be best if you chose not to become a so-called serious artist or any type of artist whatever, you're only letting yourself in for a life of defeats and frustration, listen to me, Martin, don't turn your back on me in that thoughtless and most annoying fashion."

Typical of my father.

Arguing himself into a corner from which there seemed no possible escape, raising questions to which there were no satisfactory answers.

And still.

I didn't see and still don't how my father could have possibly existed without his precious, his so-called genuine art, his very being in fact nothing but the being of a true, a genuine artist, yes, there was little or no getting around this annoying fact, this disturbing dilemma, my father's occasional outbursts, his impossible, unanswerable questions concerning his art and therefore his very being nothing but temporary lapses in confidence, in judgment, nothing but the usual doubts assailing everyone from time to time but true, genuine artists more than most perhaps, in other words I took these, my father's occasional outbursts as little more than temporary setbacks, certain unavoidable lapses of purpose that served to clear the air before he could return to his art, to himself that is and his single-minded pursuit of all he held near and dear, although at this stage I must confess that these occasional outbursts, these doubts of his frequently got to me as well, yes, even to the point of questioning his call, his very worth as a true, a genuine artist, not my own of course, for never in my entire life did I experience that flash, that shock of insight, of revelation my father had, in other words never in my entire life did I entertain the notion of being or even becoming a real, a genuine artist, no, from the very start art for me was no more or less than a way of communicating with my father and so with myself as well perhaps, but, as I said, his doubts frequently becoming my doubts and his impossible questions mine as well, in other words this destructive or self-destructive streak in my father affecting me in more ways than he could have possibly realized, yes, yes, I simply bided my time until it should pass, which it always did of course, that is until the very end when my father's nagging doubts, his impossible questions finally and lastingly got the better of him and his so-called real, his genuine art, and left him as if stranded outside this art as well as himself, but by that time I had become someone or something different myself, yes, both of us as if strangers to one another by then which only my subsequent memories, my unwritten recollections have a shot of curing, of setting right.

My first so-called exhibit. My only exhibit.
My works finally on display for eyes other than my father's.
It never would have materialized, and no doubt it shouldn't have

except for my father's relatively well known name and his formidable influence with a dealer acquaintance of his, a dealer who, by the way, considered himself one of my father's closest friends, although the reverse was far from the case, in his own mind my father with any number of so-called acquaintances but few if any close or even friends per se, "Anyone calling himself your friend is anything but," he once told me, "it's just a word, a by now meaningless word like love, duty, honor and even god itself, people with a way of hiding behind words, of disguising themselves through words, no, only the one who thinks, says, asserts nothing, may be your one true friend," no matter, the exhibit, my so-called exhibit of an extremely limited duration, yes, my works on view for little longer than a week or so, this as well as a number of other things were agreed upon in advance, for opening day, although that term more than a slight exaggeration, no matter, but for opening day my father had invited several critics of his acquaintance, critics who respected and even admired my father's work but for whom my father entertained neither respect nor any sort of admiration, no matter, but he wanted me to gain the experience or perhaps learn the lesson of what it meant to be dealing with critics, of having so-called critics scrutinize your works, "They have no more true, genuine feelings for art than does a physician, a so-called physician have for the true, the genuine pains of his patients," he told me, "but as a fledgling artist you must at least form some opinions, arm yourself with at least some salutary judgments about what it's like to deal with, and, god forbid, enter, become part of the art world," the two of us standing in a corner of the relatively small but all the same well known gallery not far from the heart of the city, "for the most part critics out for blood, like sharks they can smell and taste blood three, four, perhaps even five miles, off, no matter, for the fledgling artist any publicity is better than none, that is if he is intent on entering and in some fashion surviving in the so-called art world," which had never been my intention of course, not then, not ever, but just in case my father out to teach me a lesson he thought I needed to learn and make some use of at some future date, "for the most part critics nothing but thoughtless, wanton destroyers, employing nothing but thoughtless, wanton destruction to advance their own careers with little or no regard for the artist's own," my father needn't have worried, the critics who responded to my father's invitation attended primarily or even solely for my father's sake and not mine, in other words they were there to exchange whatever few words they could with someone who by then was relatively well known as both a genuine as well as a most reclusive artist, in other words they paid me and my rather esoteric and extremely limited works of art the scantest attention while focusing most of their time and energies on attempting to penetrate my father, the so-called true, the genuine artist, as a matter of fact nothing was ever written about me or my works by those or any other critics then or in the future, which was fine, really, absolutely fine with me although, even though he never admitted, it irritated my father, by the end of the week I had sold one, yes, just a single work at a ridiculous and even insulting sum, yes, no doubt bought by someone who had not the least notion of true, of genuine art, someone who had simply and accidentally wandered into the gallery and couldn't resist a deal, a bargain purchase, "Well, at least you've sold your first painting, Martin," my father smiled afterwards, no doubt trying to make light of the situation, but he and I both knew, and this even before the exhibit, that I wasn't nor was I destined to become a true, a genuine artist, no, not even a second, third or even a fifth-rate artist, that all my so-called, sketches, drawings and partings were simply and only intended to communicate with my father, meant as communication devices with my father, but neither of us ever discussed or even alluded to this aspect of my so-called art, in other words after my one and only exhibit we carried on the same as before, working side by side the same as before, and this more or less suited our purposes, his as well as mine, although by then my father with strong and ever increasing doubts about the price demanded of genuine artists, for their becoming and being so-called true and genuine artists, in other words, and looked at in a certain way, by arranging my first and only exhibit and teaching me the lesson of my first and only exhibit, my father simply looking out for my interests which by then and according to him lay somewhere other than in becoming and being a so-called genuine artist, in other words, and this is just a mere guess on my part, by then my father no longer wished for me what he had all his life wished for and achieved himself, that of becoming and then continuing to be a genuine artist, but as I say this is mere conjecture, guesswork on my part and comprehensible only in the light of then future now past events, in other words it is no easy matter to distinguish between what I felt and thought then and what I think and feel now, in some ways it's best not to even attempt it and let memory lead me where it will without imposing my present thoughts and feelings on those of the past.

"Shut your eyes," my father commanded. "Open, shut, open them. Shut them."

My father never missing an opportunity to impart what he termed certain necessary lessons, in this case the simplest and most necessary one of looking, observing, of truly seeing, "Open them now. Shut them now," we were looking at a painting by Matisse, his 'Piano Lesson' if I'm not mistaken, because of the time of morning the two of us alone in that hall, that part of the museum devoted to the so-called moderns, a term my father detested, as he detested all labels, all so-called schools applied to true, to genuine artists, "No real artist ever labels himself," he had told me, "places himself in any sort of category, no, he simply paints or sculpts or carves according to the dictates of his genius," no matter, but we were standing in front of Matisse's 'Piano Lesson' with my father trying to teach me how to look at and truly see Matisse's 'Piano Lesson,' "Open your eyes, Martin, shut them, open them," my father trying to teach me the difference between outer and inner visions but also the alliance, the necessary fusion between them, at least when it came to certain real, certain genuine works of art, "You, Martin, listen to me, you must reach a point, a state where your outer and inner visions act, see as one, this is absolutely essential when confronted with a work like Matisse's 'Piano Lesson,' Matisse's 'Piano Lesson' can only fully and truly reveal itself when viewed through both the outer and inner eye," I looked away, it was but a momentary affair, a brief lapse in concentration, Matisse's 'Piano Lesson' on the verge of mesmerizing me, "Please, Martin, please, don't make me feel I'm wasting my breath, my time with this," we resumed then, I with my looking and listening and my father with his looking and lecturing, "You see, Martin, you see, it's the very least you can do given that Matisse created, worked with both his outer and inner eyes, a painting like this would make absolutely no sense unless both created and viewed through the outer and inner eye, yes, only if you can see, experience Matisse's world as he saw, experienced and subsequently created it can you claim that you not only understand but truly experience it, with other artists, other so-called second, third and fifth rate artists there is absolutely no need for this, other so-called second, third and fifth rate artists neither demand nor expect such close scrutiny, they paint with strictly the outer and not the inner eye, listen to me, Martin, they paint what they paint only through their outer eyes and never, listen, never their inner ones, their art in this sense is a tawdry, miserable and absolutely meaningless affair, they have no real vision to speak of, no true inner vision I'm talking of, and therefore demand none from you, none from their viewers, no, they are perfectly satisfied in presenting you with a simplified and therefore terribly distorted and distorting vision of so-called reality, they are nothing more than false and distorting mirrors in which they expect their viewers to see the world, to see themselves that is, yes, in much the same or even exactly the same way they view and perceive themselves, these false, these phony and therefore most destructive artists I'm talking of, but then you have Matisse, someone like Matisse and his glaringly real, his endlessly analyzable 'Piano Lesson,' do pay attention if at all possible, Matisse who lays bare not just what is out there but in here as well," and at this point my father struck his chest in a most forceful fashion, "because our vision, our true, collective and therefore genuine vision consists not only of what's out there or of what we think is out there but of what's in here as well," and again my father struck his chest, although a bit less forcefully this time, "yes," he nodded, "yes, through his very own simplicity, his flatness of shapes and forms as well as his choice of colors with which not even Picasso could compete, no matter, but through all these he effectively distorts the world but only in order to reveal it, whereas others, your so-called second, third and fifth rate artists merely attempt to reveal the world while doing nothing more than distort, it, yes, Matisse, someone like Matisse with the greatest, the most amazing simplicity inside himself, in other words he understood, absolutely understood that it is only through this inner simplicity that one can view and hopefully comprehend as well as communicate the awesome complexity of the world, of life all around, yes, and he understood something else as well, that in and through time, but eventually beyond time, outer and inner visions not only blend, not only fuse but are recognized, yes, absolutely recognized as being one and the same, yes, and it's from this absolute recognition with its ensuing energy, its strength that he proceeds to paint, to carve, to sculpt, whatever, yes, and thereby he imports to his viewers, some at any rate, the same absolute recognition and strength through which to view, yes, to see the so-called world" which includes themselves of course, yes," my father seized me by the shoulder, "Matisse forever assaulting, grabbing and even temporarily confusing us but all in order to ultimately free us to allow our unobstructed and bracing view of the world, of ourselves that is, and this is something none of your so-called second or third or fifth rate artists are capable of doing, and even if they were they would still lack the absolute drive, the passion to even attempt it, no," my father suddenly stepped forward, turned and stared at me instead of Matisse, Matisse's 'Piano Lesson,' "your second, your third, your fifth rate artists so-called reveal in order to mask, whereas Matisse masks simply to reveal," he stopped talking, lecturing then, almost as though he abruptly encountered and recognized the futility of words, suddenly heard the prolonged and confusing symphony of his own words, silence, yes, once again silence overwhelming us both, although the source of his silence different from mine I was sure, his issuing from his having worked through and beyond words and mine from simple exhaustion as well confusion, I don't know how long we stood there just looking, staring at one another, Matisse and his 'Piano lesson' gone from our minds by then, although not entirely, with something, I don't know what, but something else taking its place, but the feeling I had at the time, and all this in hindsight, in retrospect, was of a kind of dizziness, nausea even as if after a physical assault, Matisse's as well as my father's of course, and I could hardly wait for that dense, my dense and impenetrable silence to pass, for both of us to finally move, walk away, to leave the museum behind.

I have terrific conversations with my father now.
Now, not then.
My father never what one might call a real, a natural listener, a real, a genuine artist of course but never a real, a genuine listener, or perhaps his so-called listening consisted only of his listening to, of his hearing and overhearing himself, I on the other hand a true, a genuine listener, although not through choice, no, I don't think so, but through sheer necessity, in other words throughout our life together my father spoke and I listened, and never, almost never the other way around, different now, of course, now that he's gone, my father with no choice but to listen and I to speak in a manner of speaking, yes, as I said we have terrific conversations, astounding one way conversations with speaker and listener the opposite of what they were before, it's curious, but I now find I have so much to say, to reveal to him even or especially since he has no way of responding but only of listening, I find it quite simple and easy to unburden myself, to start with just one thought that quite naturally, almost effortlessly generates the next and the one after, 'All artists,' I tell him, 'even our so-called real, our genuine artists are nothing but impostors, fakes in the end,' yes, it does my heart good to be able to express myself in this fashion even though at times I can hardly escape the feeling that not only the voice but even the contents of what I'm saying are still his in some way, 'An artist,' I tell him, 'even a true, a genuine artist is nothing but an abject hack and embarrassing failure in the end,' yes, how I've been longing for years now to tell him this even though on more than one occasion he told me, himself the very same thing, 'Real, genuine art all around us,' I tell him, 'there is no, absolutely no need for so-called

true artists to exemplify, to illustrate this,' I study his face, stare into his eyes as I say this, his face still and always in front of me, his face with its varied and various expressions, it takes little or no effort on my part to conjure it up, as a matter of fact I often imagine, feel him accomplishing this conjuring himself, 'In their unceasing attempts,' I tell him, 'to create artificial worlds to substitute for the real one, genuine artists causing nothing but harm to themselves and to others,' my father nods without either agreeing or disagreeing, 'Yes,' I tell him, 'it's better to have artists of less talent and ambition who because of their limited visions cause limited damage as well,' my father coughs, clears his throat, 'All so-called visions, even those of just light and colors cause unnecessary confusion and irreparable harm in the end,' my father smiles and gestures, I'm not giving up, he has nowhere to go and I demand his unwavering attention, 'True, genuine artists do nothing but pour acid, uric acid into the eyes of their viewers,' my father longing to disappear then, nothing doing, I am the one calling the shots now, the one to talk and he to listen.

I exhaust myself.

One-sided conversations with my father no easy matter, even with my doing the talking and he the listening.

I shut my eyes to dismiss him.

I see little reason to continue, not now, some other time perhaps.

I both love and hate the old bastard, the once but no longer true and genuine artist, yes, I both love and hate him still.

"Let's talk about your true, your genuine visionaries," my father was saying, "let's discuss Goya for a spell."

We were visiting a gallery exhibiting, selling some of Goya's works, "As with most genuine artists," my father told me, "a number of their works disappear, reappear only to disappear once more, swallowed whole, once again consigned to practical oblivion by the greed of so-called collectors."

The dealer, the so-called art dealer standing but a few steps behind us, now and again he commented, uttered a few explanatory words my father did his best to disregard, no, my father would not give this so-called art dealer the satisfaction of actually turning about and facing him, of conducting any sort of conversation with him, no, my father and I here simply to view and discuss a few lost and found Goyas, in other words my father here simply to lecture and I to listen, my father in no mood to put up with any sort of interference, any sort of verbal interference, the dealer soon realized this, sized up the situation that presented itself, he kept quiet after awhile while still remaining where he was, where he stood, just waiting, biding his time until my father should finish his monologue, his lecture to the young man beside him.

"Goya an artist," my father was saying, "yes, a genuine artist with a vision. Dangerous of course, in this world nothing more dangerous for a true artist than to have a genuine vision, to paint as well as to survive armed with nothing but his vision, that Goya managed, although at times less well than at others, but that he actually managed for as long as he had is nothing short of amazing, that this menacing world didn't destroy him sooner than it had, chew him to bits and spit him out as if on the spot, as soon as he had finished and exhibited his first so-called visionary work is nothing short of amazing."

We were standing in front of one of Goya's etchings, one of his lost and found etchings, with my father occasionally raising his arm, extending his arm as if reaching for the work, not possible of course as we stood several feet from the etching and carefully maintained this distance throughout his lecture.

The etching itself needing few if any explanations, its effect of horror at once immediate and penetrating, still, my father persisted, he could not resist the temptation to lecture, to attempt the impossible task of translating the image into words.

"A kind of simplicity here as well, Martin, although of a shocking, brutal and dreadful sort. Note the power, the strength of the lines, they strike the viewer with enough force to bring him to his knees without permitting him the opportunity to shut his eyes, no, face-to-face with a work, an etching like this the viewer with no choice but to keep his eyes wide open and continue staring ever deeper into the abyss that was Goya's vision and becomes our own as well."

My father taking a deep breath, as if inhaling the work, inhaling Goya's vision.

"A ghost, an apparition, a phantom," he continued. "See its tremendous, its impossible size, its magnificent but horrifying dimensions, see how it extends its arms, how it hovers over that bleak and devastated landscape where all life has been extinguished, where nothing will ever flourish again, yes, Goya pulled no punches as far as his art, his vision was concerned, through his art, his vision Goya ready to take on all comers, all challengers here, yes, here was an artist with absolutely no delusions or illusions, who worked with absolutely no illusions or delusions, and armed with what, I'm asking you, Martin, armed with only his vision and immense talent of course, that goes without saying, but his incredible vision of a merciless, destructive world, a world bent on destruction instead of creation, whose very essence is nothing but destruction instead of creation, and this, yes, to his eternal credit, this was Goya's true and genuine vision, his unflinching gaze and penetration of the evils all around, and note, please, note, Martin, that 'evils' is always plural while 'beauty,' true, genuine beauty always singular, no matter, and this, this particular etching by Goya the perfect depiction of the former, yes, not even Picasso's 'Guernica' comes close, and one cannot, no, absolutely cannot depict these sorts of evils without a true knowledge and appreciation of real, genuine beauty, which Goya did of course, no one better than he, but in this instance, in this etching his main and only concern with the evils all around, the perfect subjects for his darkest visions which like a whirlpool seize and pull us down into the very depths of hell."

My father finished.

The dealer waited, bided his time before making his approach, he walked softly on the wooden floor so we could barely hear his approach, yes, we finally became aware of his presence only when he was standing right beside us, "I can see you're serious," he practically whispered, "genuine worshippers of art," my father wincing at the words as well as the tone, "If you'd like we could discuss the provenance as well as the inestimable worth of a work like this," my father glared at him with an icy stare, searching, yes, I knew that look of my father's that gave him sufficient time to search for and find the appropriate words, having found them his expression changed, the glaring stare turned into a benevolent smile, "Excuse us," he replied in measured tones, "but we are here merely to admire and appreciate Goya, not to bargain about him."

We left the gallery.

Exited like theater goers after a questionable performance.

My father often appears in my dreams.

Now, not then.

When I was working, living with my father there was no need, no, absolutely no need for me to dream about him, for him to enter my dreams, living, working with him enough of a dream at the time, to actually dream about him was totally unnecessary, it would have simply complicated, confused an already complicated and confusing situation, no, my so-called father-

dreams occurring now only as if to supplement and even simplify my daily, my hourly thinking about him.

He paints in my dreams.

What else?

I stand alongside him the same as back then, only this time I'm not working, painting the way he is, that is in a ridiculous, useless and even pathetic imitation of the way he was, this time, in my current dreams that is, I simply stand and observe, there is absolutely no pretense about doing anything other than standing and observing, now as so often back then my father hardly aware of my presence, my father lost in his work, the same now as back then.

No lectures.

My father finally dead to words in my dreams, 'The dead incapable of speaking,' I often tell, remind myself, although not of working, of painting, that is if they were once so-called true, so-called genuine artists.

Occasionally he pauses, looks up.

But the pausing, the looking also part of his working, his painting, there is no separation between them, the same now as back then.

Does he actually see me? Do the dreamed actually perceive their dreamers?

Terrific question.

Better still, are the dead ever aware of the living?

For my sake I hope they're not.

Any contact, any dealings between the living and the dead a strictly one sided, one way affair, anything else would be not only bewildering but hopeless as well.

I watch and observe him without being watched and observed in turn.

I no longer see or even attempt to see the products of his labors, his so-called genuine works of art, yes, there is no reason to suppose that painting in my dreams now my father would produce anything other than true, genuine works of art the same as he did back then, but as a dreamer in the present I'm no longer interested in my father's so-called real and genuine works of art, no, the man, only the man interests me now and this in spite of my realization of how difficult if not impossible it is to separate the one from the other.

I watch his every move and gesture, do my best to let nothing about my father's appearance escape me, and this, the man I'm talking about, yes, let me make this absolutely clear, only and strictly the man and not the painter, that is in my dreams my interest in the painter consigned to oblivion, my dreams, yes, all my dreams attempting to resurrect, to recreate the man and not the painter, to in some fashion get at the man while totally disregarding the so-called painter, after all have I or have I not lived nearly all my life with the painter while hardly ever with the so-called man, solving some sort of mystery, secret about the man and not at all that of the painter, 'And just what do you intend to accomplish with all this, Martin?' I often ask myself in my dreams, a true, a genuine question if ever there was one, but it's only on waking, only when awake that I'm able to formulate some sort of an answer, yes, 'In trying to uncover the secret, the mystery of this man, the mystery and secret of your father, you're also after the secret and mystery of yourself,' and so far that's as far as I've taken it, the question as well as the tentative reply, so far and no farther for now.

What?

Now and again I suffer from a nagging nausea, a debilitating motion sickness in my dreams, yes, in my very dreams, which are then carried over into the waking state, yes, at least the initial waking state, useless to resist, to fight it, yes, there is nothing but to endure and watch it flower, because this, yes, this nagging nausea and debilitating motion sickness also a revelation of sorts, and while not yet the true, the genuine revelation of the mystery of my father as well as myself, it's still a part of the process, on its way to that last, that final and therefore ultimately true and genuine revelation about my father and myself, at least so I tell myself.

Yes.

In and out of my dreams.

That's what I tell myself.

"Simplicity," my father told me, "nothing but simplicity in the end as well as at the beginning."

He was suffering from mind, from body splitting headaches by then, "Genetic," he assured me, "no need for concern," but from time to time his mind, his entire body as if on fire, yet, strangely enough, it was during this period he produced his most so-called important and lasting works.

"The city," he contradicted himself, "my debilitating headaches nothing but the accumulated and delayed response to the city," he gestured.

We were out of doors once more, zigzagging through the city streets, "The very arteries of life," my father once called them, the two of us as if looking for a way in or out, impossible to say which.

"How can one possibly exist and work in the city?" he asked, "how can a so-called genuine artist survive and create in the city?"

From time to time he rushed, hurried ahead or perhaps I fell, lagged behind, but on certain streets and at certain times we managed to walk side by side, in other words I caught up with my father and his words which I was sure would have continued unabated even if I had not.

"There is nothing so fragile, so fleeting as art, while there is nothing so hard, so durable as the city. You see my point, Martin, you see the contradiction, the impossibility? An artist, a true, a genuine artist sets out to work in the city, who gets his so-called sources of inspiration from the city, eventually winds up pitting himself against the obstinate strength, the merciless destructive forces of the city, you see my point, Martin, and it's likely, yes, even quite likely that he won't recognize, realize this until it's too late, too late for him as a true, a genuine artist that is, yes, in the end the city gets the better, the best of him, and then, yes, what else is left him but endless, mind numbing repetition of his once true and genuine works, and while they may still appear as both true and genuine to the uninformed observer, they are no longer either true or genuine as far as the artist himself is concerned, in other words that initial spark, that light of creativity no longer what it once was, the city has triumphed, you see, destroyed everything worthwhile in the artist's genuine, so-called true works of art, and himself as well perhaps."

My father speaking in fairly loud although measured tones, some of the passersby turned to look, to listen to his word fragments, but this without stopping or even slowing their walks, the same as my father who neither stopped nor slowed his walk while holding forth.

"Yes, art both fragile and fleeting," he repeated, "in some of Picasso's so-called light-pencil drawings you have the perfect examples, although have is the wrong term, absolutely wrong for they vanished nearly as soon as he drew them on this glass surface, this canvas of glass, yes, Picasso out to simply please himself or perhaps to illustrate to himself and whoever was around the very fragile and fleeting nature of art."

My father stumbled, temporarily lost his balance, a crack, some sort of crack in the sidewalk he hadn't seen, my father never looking down, my father always looking up or straight ahead as he walked.

"Sooner or later an artist must decide," he continued, "yes, absolutely decide to save himself and his so-called true, his genuine art from the city's destroying clutches, in other words there comes a time, an inevitable time when sheer survival in the city is no longer feasible as far as his art is concerned, when in order to save his art he must save himself or in order to save himself he must save his art, yes, abandoning the city then his only option, the only possible answer, he must muster the courage then, if that's what it is, although it's little more than common sense, but muster the courage let's just say to leave the city for the country, to shove off one sort of existence, one sort of life in order to embrace another, his art, you see, yes, his very art as well as his sanity and physical well being demand it, there can be no more hesitation, no more playing for time, Martin, you understand what I'm saying, he must absolutely choose, decide and act as if all at once, altogether at the same time I mean, and then, afterwards I mean, there can, there must be no coming back, yes, there can be no return."

In some ways my father something of a sad and comic figure by then, although passionate, contradictorily still passionate nearly to the very end, no matter, but his very movements, lectures and even his paintings with elements of both comedy and sadness, yes, the grand although subtle comedy and sadness of this last phase of his life, which took me by surprise of course, although perhaps it didn't, hard to say at this distance in time.

My father dreaming of the country, his waking dreams increasingly about the country then, he himself could hardly tell what was and wasn't real about these so-called dreams, these meditations of the country, these dreams existing side by side with his mind and body splitting headaches caused by the city, he juxtaposed, pitted these dreams against the city's realities, these dreams like soft silhouettes to counter the city's stark realities, instead of lecturing, ranting against the city now he often told stories about the country, although those stories often germinating from his still periodic rants and raves against the city, in other words the two no separate entities by any means, even if my father wished or pretended they were.

"There are no true sunrises, sunsets or even storms in the city, all true sunrises, sunsets and even storms to be found only in the country, the same for noises, silences and the very passage of time, the only true noises, silences and even the passage of time to be had only in the country and not the city, only fake, only second-hand individuals seek them in the city and not the country, only confused and so-called restless spirits seek them in the city and not the country, the country like a haven, a refuge against all the phony enchantments of the city, in other words the enchantments of the country real whereas those of the city merely make-believe, at some stage of his so-called career a true, a genuine artist can only find by losing himself in the country and not at all the city."

His dreams, his stories about the country spinning about my head no less than his own.

"The city a confusing and dangerous place for the genuine artist, whereas the country a clear and welcoming one. The city manufactures and thrives on confusion, whereas the country creates and thrives on clarity. The most insidious danger comes from the city just as the most welcoming peace from the country. There is nothing but chaos in the city and only harmony and order in the country," and so on.

I wondered.

By then my father definitely caught in his own exaggerations, trapped by his own lying dreams or dreaming lies.

"Listen, listen to me, Martin."

And so on.

For long hours, days and even weeks my father's so-called tales about the country continued, I had no choice but to listen, did I ever have any choice but to listen, they existed in direct correlation with, took their very lives from his mind and body bending headaches, they only let up, abated when his headaches did the same, although not gone, never entirely gone, and I .sensed, I knew it was only a question of time before they should return full blown once more to finally and lastingly seize and capture him.

I listened though.

What choice but to listen?

"Listen, listen to me, Martin."

Dusk.

A pleasant, a soothing light through the kitchen window.

"The moment one desires, the moment one chooses then acts to become a so-called real, a genuine artist, does everything possible, everything in his power to turn himself into a true, a genuine artist, he is finished. Do you understand? Finished!" he pounded the table.

Our food untouched.

Our so-called supper of leftovers from the various restaurants untouched.

"Every choice, every decision, every act of a genuine artist a fake, a phony and in the end a highly destructive choice, decision and act, his very choosing and then acting, working as a genuine artist anything but genuine, real, he must become a so-called true and genuine artist not through any sort of choice and subsequent action but something altogether different, do you see, Martin, yet how can he when everything in life, throughout our so-called ordinary and artistic lives is nothing but choice and subsequent action with a debilitating gap between the two, this destructive gap of time I'm talking about, in other words as soon as an ordinary man or even an extraordinary artist chooses and subsequently acts he is finished, don't, please, don't play with that food, Martin, because what the extraordinary artist, although not the ordinary man, no, I hardly think so, but what the extraordinary artist is after is some sort of instantaneous and therefore pure and genuine action, that is action without any prior choosing and deciding, but that's impossible, Martin, do you see, and what separates the extraordinary artist from the ordinary man is that the former sees, yes, clearly and absolutely sees this impossibility while still pursuing it, the ordinary man with no such compunction, so-called necessity, but both, listen to me, Martin, both finished from the start, in other words as soon as they choose to act, to paint, to whatever, in other words as soon as they choose to live instead of simply living or painting or whatever, because life is not a matter of choice, no, absolutely not, as soon as there is choice and subsequent action both the ordinary man and the extraordinary artist are finished, do you hear, Martin, finished even as they start."

And once more my father pounded the table, although gentler, softer this time.

"And what's before the start, the beginning?" I screwed up my courage to ask.

Rarely if ever did I interrupt or ask my father any questions, I must have thought it both useless as well as ultimately destructive, but I did this time, almost without thinking.

My father looked up.

Seeing, scrutinizing me then the way he so often saw and scrutinized various works of art, in other words taking his time before deciding, formulating some sort of judgment about what lay in front of his eyes.

"Nothing," he finally replied, "absolutely nothing. Neither before the beginning nor after the end. Absolutely nothing."

As so often, no, as always before my father left the interpretation of his remarks, his dicta entirely up to me, in other words left me groping in the dark as so often, no, always before, although whether that had been his original intention I had no way of knowing.

And still don't.

"No one," my father was saying, "yes, no one captures the spirit, the entire human spirit like Rembrandt."

We were standing in front of one of one of Rembrandt's remarkable self-portraits, one of his last and therefore most accomplished self portraits, Rembrandt calling on all of his inestimable resources as an artist as well as a man to bestow upon the world this incredible map of the human spirit, of a life lived, suffered and endured, yes, still endured.

"It takes your breath away," my father was saying, my father who no longer stood stock still but found it necessary to move, now to the left, now the right in front of the portrait as if to keep himself from being fully seized, entirely overwhelmed by Rembrandt's vision.

"With the exception of Shakespeare who worked in a completely different, an entirely intellectual medium, no one has penetrated the human soul, the human psyche the way Rembrandt has."

Our visits, our so-called pilgrimages to the city's museums less and less frequent now, as a matter of fact with each visit, each so-called pilgrimage I thought, 'Yes, Martin, yes, this will be the very last,' every visit with a certain air of leave taking, of farewell about it.

My father's so-called lectures also growing less and less complicated, involved, yes, I had the definite feeling that now he was saying only what was necessary, absolutely essential while keeping the rest to himself, buried in his mind.

"In these self-portraits of his," my father was saying, "especially these last and most comprehensive ones, Rembrandt never winced, looked away nor in any way fooled or cheated, himself, which is to say he never cheated or fooled us, his viewers, yes, his unblinking stare resembling Shakespeare in this who also never cheated himself nor his audience, both men, both artists remarkably similar in this, the only difference, and it's a significant one, is that in this process, in these artistic gifts Shakespeare managed to absent, to hide himself while Rembrandt to fully expose and reveal himself, yes, one can certainly debate which is the more striking, the more effective approach, but the results achieved the same in both artists, the steadfast, the unwavering, the un-apologizing stare, which not everyone appreciates, not everyone can handle."

My father looked away.

Suddenly.

Rembrandt's gaze, his unflinching stare as if become too much for him, yes, as he turned to look at me his eyes as if mirroring Rembrandt's, yes, the distance between us never greater than then, yes, but in this distance also a kind of painful, distressing closeness, my turn to look away then, "Have we had enough?" my father asked, and he headed with his usual firm steps down the museum corridor, although I took my time before I followed, before I caught up with him.

We locked up our apartment, our so-called studio with all our paintings, my father's genuine ones along with my third, fourth and even fifth rate ones without entirely abandoning them, that is we carried them in our heads, left them behind only in the strictest physical sense, in other words we traveled light in one sense but not in another, and this even though my father pronounced that looking back was deadly, that for an artist as well as a man there was nothing more destructive than looking back, I avoided his eyes, his gaze, his eyes no longer my father's I felt, we packed light for our journey to the country, "How's this for inspiration?" my father asked, meaning the very opposite of course, the very non-inspiration of an artist turning his back on his so-called art, of his leaving his art behind, "Have you ever known of an artist, a true, a genuine artist abandoning, listen to me, Martin, willingly abandoning his so-called art, any number of cases, instances of his art abandoning him, pick up any dictionary, history of art and you'll see them faithfully recorded, but a genuine artist abandoning his genuine art, not on your life, Martin, think of Picasso, of Matisse, Martin, who created if not exactly struggled to the very end of their lives, who to the very end of their lives continued to elevate their art above and beyond everything else, in other words they allowed nothing, absolutely nothing to stop them, to interfere with their art, and I'm talking of personal as well as impersonal matters, although for great, for genuine artists the imper-sonal always becomes the personal and the other way around, but both Picasso and Matisse continuing to work, never abandoning their work even in the midst of personal as well as impersonal tragedies, of so-called specific as well as universal tragedies, think of your wars, Martin, of the world gone periodically mad with no one brave or wise or foolish or influential enough to stop them, and then the so-called private, the unavoidable tragedies of individual lives, the various hurts, betrayals and losses in individual lives, but great, grand masters like Matisse and Picasso worked through them all, the former with his useless, arthritic fingers, the latter with his practically useless, arthritic mind, no, they would let nothing stop them, with the exception of death of course, the grandest, the truest and therefore the most eloquent artist I know, but as far as I know I am the only real, the only genuine artist to ever willingly abandon, turn his back on his so-called art, in other words to opt for death in the midst of life or for life in the midst of death, and this makes me something, someone at once extraordinary as well as ordinary, amazingly extraordinary as well as liberatingly ordinary, the one better or worse than the other, impossible to say, I'd be lying if I tried."

We unpacked then.

My father's burst, his outburst of words enough to negate, to cancel our leaving, in other words his words replacing, taking the place of our actual leaving, his flood of words sufficient to derail his immediate need for change, his nearly irresistible urge to abandon, to betray one kind of life for another, the certainty of his prior existence for the uncertainty of a questionable future one, his life of an extraordinary artist for that of an ordinary non-artist that is, in other words the more things were about to change the more they were destined to remain the same, I followed him in this as in everything else, whether willingly or unwillingly, I followed him in this as in everything else.

Near blizzard conditions.

The two of us out of doors and on our way, yes, once more on our way to a museum, "Can you think of a better time, Martin, with everyone else hunkered down, refusing to abandon the safety of their homes, their apartments?" the city itself as if under siege, abandoning itself to the mindless fury of the elements, "Nature uncaring, Martin, nature forever testing, challenging us, and destroying, yes, of course, destroying us all in the end, that's why I have no patience, no, absolutely none for your so-called genre, your landscape artists, your so-called worshippers of nature who only see nature as creative and not destructive, but if one then the other, Martin, if creation then destruction, in fact destruction might well be the highest form of creation and so-called creation the highest form of destruction, but these second, third and fifth rate artists simply refuse to see, to acknowledge, and if they refuse to see, to acknowledge this in nature you can be sure they refuse to see, to acknowledge this in themselves as well, they simply blink and go on blinking in the face of so-called reality, their second, third and fifth rate art amply testifies to this, it's art created through blinking eyes not wide open ones, just as they view and create themselves through the same blinking eyes and not wide open ones."

The city's usual landmarks obstructed if not entirely erased. We walked with our heads down, looking up only from time to time to get our bearings, to establish or confirm some kind of correspondence between the map in our heads and the nearly invisible city all around.

"All light, all colors gone," my father remarked. "Yet it's under these adverse, these impossible conditions that I would love to attempt a true, a genuine painting in light and colors, an impossible and therefore ultimate painting in light and colors, and done, you understand, Martin, be forever done after that, because once one succeeds in creating such an impossible and therefore ultimate painting, there is nothing left to attempt, to try afterwards."

"Breathe slowly, deeply, Martin," my father told me later. "Each breath as though it were your last."

"Make no mistake, Martin, there is nothing kind and forgiving about either the city or the country, in this both the country and the city are the same, neither shows any kindness, any mercy, they're simply incapable. In the city you may have a fake, a sham veneer of civility but underneath there is nothing but abandon and destruction, a wanton abandon and destruction, and the country is exactly the same minus the veneer of course, the country dishes out the same, the same abandon and destruction only in a simpler, a more direct way, if anyone, any artist longs for the country to avoid abandon and destruction, because he's had enough of abandon and destruction he is merely fooling himself and whomever he might be dragging along, do you understand, Martin, it all comes back to me now, the very thing that was killing your sainted mother, the country I'm talking about, was killing me as well without my realizing it at the time, too young, too eager, too foolish to have realized it at the time, but the city with its feigningly, wide open arms and the country with its unabashedly wide open arms are both exactly the same, do you understand, Martin, in the end they both wind up seizing, grasping and choking the very life out of the sensitive soul, the so-called first rate artist, the difference only in the why not the how, in the city it's hypertension and activity that eventually turn men into beasts, turn, them against themselves and one another, in the country it's boredom, yes, sheer boredom that turns men into beasts, uncaring destroyers of themselves and others, the end result the same for the sensitive soul, the so-called first rate artist, it's useless and even harmful, yes, extremely harmful to pretend otherwise, it hardly matters where the sensitive soul, the so-called first rate artist finds himself, in the end he must simply face the fact that he belongs neither in the city nor the country, it's six of one and a half dozen of the other, the only world he truly belongs to is the one of his own making, his so-called world of art, and even that becomes troubling, questionable from time to time, even that fails to provide the kind of grounding he's longed for all his life, but I don't think you're listening, Martin, and you're breathing through your mouth not your nose, I warned you against that, I warned you against breathing through your mouth not your nose."

We ascended the snow covered stairs with packed ice underneath. As always my father careful of his footing and warning me about mine.

We entered a nearly abandoned building, works of art as if abandoned to themselves.

As we walked down the corridor toward the hall of the Impressionists my father still harping about the differences as well as the similarities, the awful similarities he called them, between the city and the country.

"The bloodthirsty cruelty, the wanton destruction the same in both, the city may destroy, kill with a smile and the country with a grimace but the destruction, the killing the same in both, the utterly despotic and merciless nature of the city little different from the utterly despotic and merciless nature of nature herself, as I said the city kills with a smile and nature with a grimace, the result the same in both, destruction and death the same with both, the city simply creates and sanctions a make-believe world with destruction and death underneath while the country forbids, yes, strictly forbids any form of pretending and makes you confront destruction and death head on as it were, your mother never realized this, yes, she absolutely refused to realize this which killed her in the end of course, I also failed to realize this, realized it only too late, after the fact as it were, but the country didn't destroy and kill me the way it did your mother, in some curious and incomprehensible fashion the country gave me my art instead, do you understand, Martin, instead of destroying and killing me the country gave me my art which I then used as a shield and weapon against the country and later the city itself, in fact against any and all comers which often included myself, but without this shield, this weapon your mother was utterly and pathetically defenseless, in other words she had only herself, her sensitive and naked soul to pit against the country's murder-ous will, and it wasn't enough, no, it never is, a naked, a sensitive soul never enough against the country's or the city's bloodthirsty assaults, a powerful, an effective shield desperately needed, like art, Martin, for me it was art, without my so-called art I would not have survived the country and later the city, yes, gone on not only to survive but to thrive in the city, but lacking my defense, my art, your mother became just another helpless and pitiful victim of the country's consuming brutali-ties, and who knows but that the same, yes, exactly the same might have happened in the city as well, I'm just guessing, Martin, but look at any city people, Martin, any with an open and defenseless heart that is and you're looking at abject, hopeless victims in the end, and this with or without their knowing it, it doesn't matter, yes, in the city as well as the country only the truly brutal survive or ones with effective weapons like so-called artists, but both the country and the city produce only three kinds of people, victims, brutes and those with effective weapons, and, let me tell you, Martin, art is the most effective weapon I know against both the city's and the country's countless cruelties, and practically all artists, especially your true, your genuine artists use their art to survive, yes, first and foremost to survive, they may very well tell themselves that they have something to share, to communicate with the rest of the world, and while that may be true up to a point, in the end it's nothing but a fairy tale they tell themselves, the main, the primary purpose of their art is survival, survival of the self I'm talking about, so-called art simply their way of coping with, of getting through life, and that's what I mean to tell you, Martin, that's what I wish to make absolutely clear."

My father working himself into a state.

Ever since his decision, his irrevocable although perhaps only temporary decision to remain in the city my father now and again working himself into a state, flooding himself with his own words to the point of nearly drowning in them, the only thing that saved him I thought at the time was his having a listener, a so-called sharer in his flood, without my presence, his so-called listener, my father would have surely drowned in his words, in the flood of his own words, or so I felt at the time.

The usual silence, a period of dense, of opaque silence followed his outburst, a kind of an antidote to the flood of words that overwhelmed us both.

It was in this dense, this all-pervasive silence that we entered the hall of the Impressionists, the Impressionists also with their own silence of course but also with their shouts of colors, light and forms, shapes that easily blended one into the other, came at you as if all at once, at a single glance, beauty, yes, all the beauty of the world carefully recorded to be presented to the eyes without the censoring, the judgmental apparatus of the brain, a direct, an immediate vision of beauty in other words at a single but comprehensive glance, both my father and I overwhelmed of course, it happened this way, yes, almost exactly in this same fashion every time we entered this hall, this so-called hall of the Impressionists, this spaceless space that still managed to suggest the immeasurable, the infinite beyond, the infectious infinite of the senses, the eyes and not at all of the mind, but even though my father was overwhelmed the same as I, how could he not have been, given his then state of mind he initially fought this immediate, this timeless beauty with all his might, with his mind that is, I could tell from the way he stood there in the middle of the hall and looked around with the least possible movement of his body, "This says nothing to our times," he whispered, "nothing to the chaos of our times," he knew he was lying of course, lying to me as well as to himself, but this was a necessary lie, a lie of the mind through which he had to find, perhaps even fight his way to a necessary and mindless truth, the immediate and unreasoning truth of the Impressionists, the apocalyptic but saving truth of the Impressionists, in the end he started to move towards them, towards all these so-called Impressionists, first towards Cezanne who wasn't an Impressionist per se but the source, the origin of all that was to follow, and then towards Renoir, Sisley, Monet and all the rest, and in front of each one he paused longer than the one before, until his pauses became nearly as immeasurable as these visions confronting him, "These Impressionists know nothing of time," he remarked, "they know only the now, the immediate, their sole concern only with the now, the immediate, but in their works they show, they teach us everything there is, everything we need to know about time itself, which is how to negate, how to sail beyond it, both time and so-called thinking intricately related, in fact they're one and the same, and these artists, these so-called Impressionists show us how to move beyond it, they confront beauty, the sheer beauty of existence more directly than any other so-called artists I know, they are the only true inhabitants of this so-called world of beauty which may well be the only world worth inhabiting and pondering, but, no, not pondering, as this world is strictly one of the senses and not at all of the mind, in other words it can't be seized but only gently, fleetingly touched even as it gently and fleetingly touches us, listen to me, Martin, no one can simply abandon, walk away from such an intoxication, eventually the viewer must hurry, practically run from such infectious beauty if he is to survive and keep on surviving in the cruel, the uncaring world all around, the viewers' defenses down, practically destroyed in the sight of such overwhelming beauty, and we all need our defenses, Martin, do you understand what I'm saying, all of us as if paralyzed, useless without our defenses, yes, the greatest danger is the proximity, the sight of such complete and uncompromising beauty, at some point the viewer must hurry, practically run from a place like this hall of the Impressionists, in other words he must come to his senses before they turn to mush and utterly destroy him, because great beauty no less destructive than ugliness, the "pervasive ugliness all around, the key to his very survival is his ongoing balance between great beauty and pervasive ugliness, so, sooner or later he must turn his back on a place like this hall of the Impressionists, hurry from it as if from a plague, do you hear me, Martin, rush from it as if from the plague itself."

At times my father quite unreasonable and extreme in his judgments, his so-called emotional and mental judgments.

He turned and hastened towards the corridor.

What choice but to follow him?

I lingered awhile, took my time but in the end what other choice but to follow him then?

"What is it," my father later asked, "to hear with one's eyes and see with one's heart? This is the question, the all-important question raised by the Impressionists, the question raised as well as answered by the so-called Impressionists, but you yourself must see, realize the inherent danger in such a question and answer, I can be of no help in this, no, none at all."

From time to time my father saying things I didn't immediately comprehend.

My father as if speaking in unfamiliar tongues as far as I was concerned.

"I was forever losing my way in the country," my father told me.

The fading light in our apartment accompanying and perhaps even birthing his words, his recollections.

"Later I never got lost in the city, with all the signs and angular streets it's practically impossible to become lost in the city, but the country another matter, an entirely different matter, and I'm not talking of the wide open fields with their practically endless visibility except in inclement weather, no, I'm speaking of the woods beyond, the woods as if at the very edge of space, yes, I would often set out for these woods, perhaps with the very intention of becoming lost in those woods, your mother failed or refused to comprehend this, on her so-called outings she kept strictly to the wide open fields, made sure, do you understand, always made sure to remain within sight and easy reach of our farmhouse, our so-called dacha, the idea of heading towards the distant woods with the possibility of becoming lost in those woods anathema to her, she failed to realize that by fearing becoming lost she was already lost, do you see, Martin," my father gestured, "and lost in a much more definitive and lasting way, there is nothing worse than being lost in a wide open field where being lost is the last, the farthest thing on one's mind, while the feeling more intense, being lost in the woods is always temporary provided one doesn't panic of course, stops from time to time to fully experience, to surrender to this measureless feeling of being lost, but your mother would have none of this, she simply didn't have it in her, the last thing she wanted to face was this feeling of being apparently irretrievably lost, so I always set off for the woods by myself, your mother always staying behind in the fields or even within the very walls of our farmhouse, whenever I set off for the woods we always said our goodbyes as though they were our last goodbyes, in other words I as if abandoning your mother and she in her turn abandoning me, neither of us willing to compromise on this for the other's sake, I simply headed for the woods and your mother merely stayed behind."

Through these recollections of his my father simply stalling, playing for time, taking a much needed break from his by now painfully intense work with light and colors, during this interim period between his initial decision to leave the city for the country and his second but just as definitive decision to remain just where he was, where we were, he was working, painting as if with a vengeance, my father turning himself against his art or his art against himself, and this even as he continued to work at a furious, a maddening pace, by then I could no longer keep up with him of course, I couldn't even pretend to be copying, imitating him, but it was during this interim period of doubts, decisions or doubtful decisions that my father produced some of his most intense and lasting works, in fact some of his most personal works, but not without his occasional pauses, his playing for time in the form of recollections of his time in the country before he became a true, a genuine artist, before the country turned him into a true and genuine artist.

"Everything seemed possible as well as impossible in the woods," he continued. "Are you listening, Martin? Both possible as well as impossible in the woods. I entered the woods unarmed, Martin, please, try to appreciate, totally unarmed as I penetrated the woods. The world, the ordinary world as if left behind, all notions of safety, security of the ordinary world abandoned, left behind, do you understand, Martin, a large chunk, perhaps even all of what I was and would ever become abandoned, left behind, there could be no, absolutely no fakery in the woods, all fakery, all fake notions of the self abandoned, left behind, and, trust me, there is only fakery, only fake notions as far as the self is concerned, and this regardless of who and what you are, yes, who and what you think you might be, yes, even so-called true and genuine artists equipped with nothing but fake notions of themselves, of who and what they might be, and on entering the woods I wasn't even one of those, not yet what one might call a true and genuine artist, no matter, but as I said the minute I entered the woods I entered a world radically different from any other I had ever known and inhabited, in other words the feeling that I both did and didn't belong to the woods im-possible to shake, silence, yes, a certain silence I had never experienced before, and this in spite of the intermittent noises of the smaller and, I assumed, larger and more distant animals all around, in other words the minute I entered the woods I entered a deep silence that no amount of intermittent noises disturbed, in fact those noises part of that overall silence if you know what I mean, Martin, and the deeper I penetrated into the woods the more fully I abandoned, left myself behind, getting, becoming lost then no great matter, I fully expected and perhaps even welcomed it, please, try to comprehend, Martin, all movement without and none within then, difficult to explain, to put into words, but no routes, no paths in those woods, it's important you realize this, after awhile I simply stopped and sat down, on a fallen tree as I recall, the tree no doubt felled by a recent storm, by a combination of high winds and intense lightning, and I sat there for quite a spell, yes, spell the most accurate description, and my only wish, if it can be called that, but my only desire was for this feeling of being completely lost to last, to continue forever if at all possible, which it didn't of course, how could it have, sooner or later I got up and began to retrace my steps, no, not retrace but simply to find a way out of the woods, which I eventually did of course, heading in just one single, one specific direction I always found my way out of the woods, and whether near or far from our farmhouse, our so-called dacha hardly mattered, the main thing was I always found my way out of those woods."

My father stopped abruptly.

Returned to his work with light and colors as though his memories, his verbal memories belonged to someone other than the true, the genuine artist, yes, the true, the genuine artist as if put on hold, waiting in the wings while my father took this detour of memories, of verbal memories that had absolutely nothing to do with the real, the genuine artist.

"What is culture, Martin," my father asked, "what is so-called civilization?"

He had just refused an interview with a reporter from one of the most influential art journals, sent him packing, this pretentious young man with impeccable diction and suit and tie to match, practically closed the door on him without ever bothering to invite him into our apartment, our so-called studio, taking the young man somewhat or even completely by surprise I needn't add, "Here," my father explained afterwards, "yes, here was someone who would never take no for an answer, whose very appearance and manner suggested that he had not gotten to where he was in life by ever having taken no for an answer, no, I could not afford to be kind to him, he was bound to misunderstand the least bit of courtesy, the minute such a young man would even set foot in our apartment he would be bound to explore, to push to the limit, no, such a young man, such an interviewer would not be satisfied until he penetrated all my so-called secrets, all the so-called secrets of my art which he never truly cared about nor in any way attempted to comprehend, no, the only reason for this kind of penetration was its subsequent exposition, its revelation to the so-called world of art, no, such a young man a most dangerous envoy, a harmful representative of the generally dangerous and harmful world at large, a world that knows only how to take without giving, how to steal without making any sort of compensation."

My father losing his train of thought.

It happened more and more frequently, my father as if starting down one road, setting off in one particular direction only to suddenly abandon it for the sake of another, and then the difficult if not impossible return, it reminded me of his stories about the woods, of his becoming, being lost in the woods, but, according to him, in the woods he had always found his way back out, and now too I had to assume some kind of backtracking, a return to his original road, his first topic under consideration.

"What is culture, what is civilization?" he demanded once more. "It is a fake, a sham, a subterfuge against the very elemental forces of nature, something to hold us captive, to keep us safe from the very elemental forces within, so-called culture, so-called society nothing but a trap to keep us from truly facing ourselves, are you listening, Martin, and all this for the sake of some notion of safety which doesn't exist, not to be found anywhere at all, least of all in a so-called culture, a so-called civilization, in fact there is nothing more dangerous and ultimately destructive than this fake, this sham notion of safety, listen to me, Martin, there is no such thing as safety anywhere at all, in death, yes, only in death perhaps, and if you for a minute think there is, that there might be safety in our so-called inner worlds you'd be sadly, grievously mistaken, the chaos within nothing but a reflection of the chaos without just as the chaos without nothing but a reflection of the chaos within, seek any sort of safety, Martin, and you'll only become a conforming and conflicted individual, a conforming and confounded artist, there are no escapes, Martin, do you understand what I'm telling you, all escapes useless, all escapes from something into something else which are basically no escapes at all, the sooner you understand this the better off you'll be, that there are basically no escapes, no safety to be found anywhere at all."

My father playing a dangerous game with me, with himself.

My father as if pulling the rug out from all reasonable as well as

unreasonable approaches to art, to life, and this in spite of his producing his most intense, his most vibrant works of art, his most personal
works of art as if in spite of, in contradiction to himself.

"In the city everything is analysis," he finished like a coda, one
of his endless refrains, "even so-called city art is nothing but analysis
of art, whereas in the country all analysis ceases, nature herself beyond
any and all analysis, those who try find themselves destroyed, ground to
dust by the; very thing they're attempting to analyze, no, nature takes no
prisoners, all prisoners taken by the city, by society, the country, nature
herself reducing everything to nothingness in the end, no thingness, do
you understand, Martin, in the country there is nothing but movement,
motionless movement, Martin, and this movement consumes everything, destroys everything in the end."

My father dreamed of the country.

My father had always been a light and easily disturbed sleeper,
his sleep no more than a pause, a respite from his real life, his true, his
genuine work in light and colors, but now his dreams, his dreams of
the country took on altogether different dimensions and importance,
in fact an importance to set against and rival his intense work in light
and colors, my father as if rushing into his dreams now the way he still
rushed into his work with light and colors, the two worlds in diametrical
opposition I felt with my father hanging in the balance, caught, seized
by now one world, now the other, rushing now into one world, now the
other.

He talked of Blake then, the poet as artist or the artist as poet, but
the artist who most forcefully blended dreams and reality in his works,
the artist who shattered all boundaries between reality and dreams more
effectively than anyone else my father could think of.

"Blake, listen to me, Martin, Blake the only true seer in the world
of art, the only one to merge his dreams with reality in his art which is
what a true seer does after all, he blends reality and dreams as though
they were a single and not two separate, two disconnected worlds, and
even though I consider myself a true, a genuine artist, never have I nor

will I ever achieve what Blake has accomplished, which is this fusion, this melting of two disparate worlds, the world of dreams and that of reality."

My father gestured expansively in the stale air of our apartment, our so-called studio.

"Yes, Blake a true seer," my father continued, "the genuine article, now and then Theotocopoulos, the so-called El Greco, comes near, approaches but in the end not even he rivals Blake's dream-like visions, his visionary dreams, to the end El Greco remains a mannered artist, an artist more of style than substance, whereas Blake is all substance as well as style, style and substance inseparable in Blake, which is precisely why he is so impossible to pigeonhole, to categorize, a few, yes, perhaps a few misguided critics have attempted it but none have convincingly succeeded, impossible to pigeonhole, to categorize dreams as art and art as dreams, they swivel inside your mind as well as your body, your mind-body or body-mind as it were, and this is also why Blake is so woefully underrepresented, practically non-existent in our museums, the Tate in London with the only so-called decent collection, but here is what I'd like to do, Martin, it's time for our break at any rate, here's what I want to do. We'll set out for one of our walks through the city, head for our so-called most prestigious museum, are you following, Martin, but we won't go in, no, this time we'll stop, sit on the very steps to this so-called prestigious museum, and then, yes, we'll search for our Blakes, our imaginary, non-existent Blakes in this museum, and it'll be both difficult and easy, difficult because it will be just an imaginary search but easy because in our imaginations this museum, this most prestigious museum will house nothing but Blakes, do you understand, Martin, the entire museum dedicated to nothing but Blakes, and then we'll take our time, on this imaginary search we'll take our imaginary time, in fact pause for an eternity in front of each imagined yet specific Blake, because Blake himself worked from and through the eternal, are you with me, Martin, in other words bringing the timeless into time and time into the timeless, and we'll stay put, remain forever in this timeless time, this eternal museum, I hope you have some idea of what I'm after, it'll be one hell of an exercise of our imaginations, the best we've ever conducted."

Was I to take my father seriously?

Was he in his right wrong mind or wrong right one by then?

We dressed quickly for our walk.

In the enveloping fog, the city winter fog we headed for the museum.

"Fogs in the city," my father later lectured, "your so-called city winter fogs not at all like your country fogs, your so-called country winter fogs."

We were sitting as if suspended in our apartment, our furniture along with our work, our canvasses as if suspended as well.

My father's words with a weightlessness that freed everything else from gravity's grasp.

"Unlike country fogs your city fogs never entirely envelop, they only partially and temporarily disorient if that, the city resists, combats its fogs the way of an army, an immense army defending its homeland, the country forever defenseless, forever open to the so-called assaults of nature, it welcomes the fog with open arms, surrenders fully to this so-called country winter fog, needless to say your mother always stayed indoors and I out during these country winter fogs, on more than a few occasions I even headed for the woods, made my way the best I could into the woods, navigated by instinct as it were, and the woods too welcoming the fog with open arms the same as the fields, everything in the woods becoming, turning into fog then, the very trunks and limbs of trees turned into fog trunks and fog limbs, the occasional collisions with these fog, these phantom trees nothing but fog and phantom collisions, the nature, do you see, Martin, the true fog and phantom nature of the world as if fully exposed and revealed then, the notion of being lost as meaningless as being found then, no difference between being lost and found in those fogs, those phantom woods, but I'm about to tell you something else, something birthed by the fog but without completely, entirely belonging to it, a boy, a young man who suddenly appeared and practically collided with me, just as I suddenly appeared and collided with him, neither of us sought nor expected such an appearance and near collision, in other words it just happened without any fore or subsequent afterthought, nothing, do you understand, nothing one second and the next this boy, this young man directly in front of me, and the same for him I was sure, nothing one second and the next this man directly in front of him, it was at once the most natural as well as unnatural thing in the world, both natural and unnatural at once."

My father paused to take a deep breath as if to ground, to anchor himself but this breath only made him lighter and less not more resistant to gravity.

"I had seen him before of course but always at a distance in the fields, a neighbor's son I was sure and something of a wanderer like myself, but his wanderings always taking him in one direction and mine in another.

"But then there he was, do you understand, Martin, there, directly in front of me."

My father paused once more but this time without taking a deep breath, holding, retaining his breath as if holding, retaining his words.

"We said nothing," he continued, "stood still and said nothing. At any rate what was there to say, what could we have said under these peculiar, these unusual circumstances, in this dense, impenetrable fog? And both of us like fog, like phantom creatures, he to me and I to him, do you understand, Martin, yet both of us fully and entirely ourselves, I can't emphasize this strongly enough, both of us fully and entirely ourselves."

My father's tale with the quality of a dream.

My father as if pulling me into one of his dreams about the country.

"The boy, the young man a deaf-mute, Martin, the same as I at the time perhaps, only he the genuine article, a true deaf-mute while I only a pretend, a make-believe one to suit the occasion. The country produces all sorts of physical as well as mental aberrations, no one can exist for long in the country without manifesting any number of physical as well as mental aberrations, but this boy, this young man, nameless, of course, nameless, but of the most fortuitous and blessed sort, his silence, Martin, his total and absolute silence which was what I needed at the time and he the same perhaps, a completely, an absolutely silent companion, he in a choiceless fashion and I in a determined one, we met frequently afterwards, nothing prearranged, Martin, no, we simply sensed, knew when and where to meet, whether by day or night, in the open fields or some spot in the dense woods, "Where are you off to?" your mother would ask, but I never responded, never bothered to explain, I would simply dress and leave our farmhouse, our so-called dacha, like a sleep, a dream walker, Martin, moving as if through a dream, and this boy, this young man would be sure to appear, this young man sure to be waiting for me or I for him, and neither of us ever knew or even questioned whether the other was real or not, I mean real enough in one sense of course, but in another, no, we simply didn't know, yes, and about the only thing we shared, had in common was our mutual silence, his real of course and mine fake, but fake in the truest, most genuine sense, and it was in and through this all encompassing silence that we walked through the fields or cut through the woods, this incomparable, this never to be repeated feeling of heading nowhere with this deaf-mute boy, this deaf-mute young man, we walked along the very edge of space and time then, I just hope you understand, Martin, yes, nothing held us back or urged us on, we simply moved the way sleepwalkers, dreamwalkers move, walk along, both of us as if suffering from a sleeping or waking sickness difficult to diagnose, to pin down, for the most part we walked side by side but occasionally the boy, the young man advanced and I followed or I advanced and he followed, we held countless conversations, countless wordless but all the more deep and meaningful conversations, this so-called relationship of ours, although it was both more and less than a normal, an ordinary relationship, but our so-called relationship lasted no more than a few months, and then we no longer met, he was out there of course the same as I but he simply failed to find me and I him, we never saw each other again, Martin, and to this day not a day goes by that I don't think of him, wonder what became of this deaf-mute boy, this deaf-mute young man, my once silent but most eloquent companion, he is a man by now, a deaf-mute old man although not nearly as old as I, but I still wonder about him, Martin, and what it would be like to run into him again, close to impossible of course, but that doesn't keep me from wondering about it the way one always wonders about the impossible and rarely, hardly ever the possible, and you may well question the reality of this so-called episode of my life in the country before I became a true and genuine artist, before the country or I myself turned myself into a true and genuine artist, I do myself of course, but there are realities and realities, Martin, but this was one of the highest, most intense order, even though to this day I persist in questioning it, questioning the very nature as well as the so-called reality of this episode in my life,"

My father bleary-eyed.

He stared at me as if through a fog, as if trying to decipher my identity, to come to some sort of conclusion about the very nature of our relationship.

The past with certain echoes, memories with certain echoes, one must be careful in listening, in interpreting them, all interpretations doomed to fail in the end, which doesn't mean one ever stops trying, with nothing but time on one's hands one can hardly stop trying to erect viable structures in which to house the past, the often disjointed and conflicting events of the past.

My father doesn't make it easy for me.

Yes, in life as well as in death my father doesn't make it easy for me.

Memories of my father nearly inextricable from memories of his true, his genuine works of art, from art in general in fact, yet the attempt must be made if I am to ever rescue, to come to terms with the man and not just the so-called real and genuine artist, it's quite an operation, a prolonged, protracted and uncertain operation requiring all my wits about me which is not always, no, certainly not always the case, the mind wanders, needless to say, frequently takes off in directions of its own choosing, I have to exert myself, marshal my dwindling resources to pull it back, return it to the task at hand, namely the rescue of my father the man with the consequent obliteration of my father the artist, the so-called true and genuine artist, but perhaps it will be the other way around, the artist lastingly rescued and the man forever condemned, too soon to tell, the operation, this so-called psychological surgery may well be successful with the patient dying, or the patient, the so-called true and genuine artist, continuing to thrive with the operation a miserable failure, I expect no help with this, I am completely on my own with this so-called psychological surgery, but I am determined to finish it once and for all, to reach some sort of understanding at or even beyond the very limits of my understanding.

"Few," my father once told me, "very few even so-called real, genuine artists ever push beyond the limits, the very limitations of their art, set themselves the task of moving beyond their art, beyond them- selves that is, in every so-called true and genuine artist an overwhelming fear of coming face to face with nothingness, of everything they hold near and dear which in their case is art of course, or both the art as well as the artist, they think it frightening as well as inconceivable to employ their art for the sake of that art's ultimate destruction, just as they think it both frightening as well as inconceivable to use themselves for their own ultimate destruction, yet when I started out, when I had my first inkling of the possibility of becoming a true and genuine artist, I already suspected or even knew that at some stage of my so-called career I would have to move, to push beyond the limits, the limitations of my art as well as myself, and that in that process I would most certainly be destroying my art as well as myself, and whatever I've accomplished in my life it was always with this horrible yet beautiful notion in the back of my mind, that all so-called creation, even creation of the highest order will and must end in nothing but its own destruction in the end, that at some stage of my so-called career the urge to move beyond, to embrace nothingness would become too strong to combat, become irresistible in fact, and in an odd, even contradictory fashion this is what kept me going, working all these years, that at some point in my life, my artistic life I'm talking about, all my efforts would bear the fruit of their own destruction, which was something I both longed for and feared, do you understand, Martin, both feared and longed for."

The same with me now?

This longing as well as fear of pushing beyond the limits as far as my father the man and the artist is concerned?

I have my good days and bad.

Days when I feel in complete control of this situation, in other words of my dead yet still living father, and others when he slips through my fingers, when this so-called enterprise of coming to terms with his life and art or his art and life as far they affected me appears both ridiculous as well as impossible.

Good days and bad.

But still I push on.

In the back of my mind some sort of limit to be reached and beyond that limit something else, something more perhaps.

Still I push on.

"I count my time," my father was saying, "my brief period with the deaf-mute boy, the deaf-mute young man as the happiest of my life."

In recounting, retelling his tale about the deaf-mute boy my father simply grasping for excuses to interrupt his work, his mind and heart breaking work of this last phase of his so-called artistic life.

The excuses multiplied even as his work progressed.

Not just his tales but noises, unexpected disturbances serving equally well, I scrutinized his every gesture as he worked while looking, hoping for some sort of disturbance, any sort of noise, the merest, shout or distant siren from the street sufficed, he stopped then, interrupted his work, broke his own concentration as though all along he had been destined to do so, to break his own concentration in other words, to interrupt his what by then had become to him his insipid work in light and colors but to me as well as subsequent viewers his most intense, his most personal work in light and colors, or in the absence of any outside disturbance, interference, he made use of his own inner disturbance and interference, his endless retelling, recounting of the tale of the young deaf-mute just one example, from time to time my father suddenly as passionate about this deaf-mute young man as he was about progressing with his most personal and intense work in light and colors.

"Such an intense," he picked up again, "such an almost unbearably close relationship as that between that boy and me, that deaf-mute young man and me can only exist between total strangers with nothing of the past or the future allowed to interfere, you understand, Martin, only strangers, total strangers without a shared past or future to interfere, yes, only strangers, total strangers capable of fully sharing the moment, the eternal now, all others only partially and hesitatingly approaching it, in order to become absolutely and painlessly, yes, especially painlessly close to someone one must first be a stranger, a total stranger to that person and he to you, much the way an artist, yes, a true, a genuine artist in order to be absolutely and painlessly close to his so-called work must first be a stranger, yes, a total stranger to that work, everything else of minor, of secondary importance, and then the silence of course, that young man's, that stranger's natural and my enforced silence also essential for the sort of relationship I'm describing, just as an artist's own inner silence also essential for his creation of true and genuine works of art, the parallel holds, Martin, even if it's not immediately evident, but artists, Martin, especially true and genuine artists, are rarely capable of forming such intense and personal relationships with anything or anyone other than their so-called art, and the same holds in reverse, people with close, with intense relationships with others rarely become true and genuine artists, ah, but are we or are we not discussing distance, distances once again, in other words closeness in one area of life means distance or distances in others, just as distance or distances in some areas of life mean closeness in another, no matter, but as I was then not yet a true and genuine artist I could well afford to be a true and genuine human being with this boy, this deaf-mute young man, the circumstances ideal for such a closeness then, yes, I have no hesitation in saying that everything worth sharing we shared back then, and shared in the only way possible, in total, in absolute silence, not even words allowed to obstruct, to interfere, do you understand, Martin, sooner or later all of us become slaves to symbols, to symbolizing, looked at a certain way art itself, even so-called great and genuine art nothing but sets of symbols, particular and peculiar ways of symbolizing, and words the same of course, nothing but sets of symbols and peculiar ways of symbolizing, in fact anything that can be said immediately ceases to be true, just as anything that can be painted, carved or sculpted immediately ceases to be true, but what I'm saying, all I'm saying is that this young deaf-mute and I were beyond all symbols, all the so-called obstacles of symbols back then, free, in other words, to become as close as we had become, closer than I had ever been or would be to another living creature in my entire life."

My father prone to exaggeration of course.

More so then than ever before, more so during these necessary interruptions to his last, his final works, these final works destined or predestined to be completed of course just as they were destined or predestined to be constantly interrupted, without these constant inter-ruptions I don't think my father could have continued, pushed himself to finish these last, these final so-called artistic statements of his, the interruptions as necessary as the work itself, the completion of the latter could not have taken place without the sporadic but continuing presence of the former.

By then I myself had ceased being a so-called artist, in other words any sort of an artist, perhaps I never had been, yes, perhaps all my life I had been nothing more than a watcher, observer and subsequent re-corder of my father's so-called artistic activities, through the years I had dedicated myself much more passionately to watching, observing and subsequently recording my father's activities than to my own so-called art, my artistic productions, in some ways ours a perfect relationship but in others, no, an unequal and most frustrating relationship as far as I was concerned, a relationship based on mutual exploitation I often thought, with most of the time my father the exploiter and I the exploit-ed but every now and again the reverse, I the exploiter and my father the exploited, but given our different personalities and differing drives perhaps our relationship had to be this way and no other, this one way and no other, I was or became my father's deaf-mute boy, his deaf-mute young man, and he the pretend deaf-mute father and artist, and this, yes, this was pretty much the way we managed to survive our lives together.

During this last, this final phase of his art my father as if under an obligation to himself and his art, an obligation to be fulfilled before he could allow himself to abandon both himself and his art, before he could embrace that total, that final freedom where no remnant of himself or his art remained.

Our apartment, our so-called studio no longer sufficiently heated, the bracing cold more suitable to our separate activities than the numbing heat, in other words my father's artistic and my watching, observing activities, in other words we already existed in the sort of silence and emptiness that would definingly and definitely seize and embrace us in the country even though weeks and even months would pass before we made that final and irreversible move, and once made it would either be the end or a brand new beginning, both of us realized, either the end or a brand new beginning to our lives, separately as well as together.

"What happens, Martin," my father asked, "what happens when an artist realizes that by pursuing his art he is approaching, bringing about an end to his art, or to a man who realizes that by his last, his final pursuit of himself he is abandoning, leaving himself behind? What happens, Martin?"

This again one of those questions to which my father expected no answers, to which there were, could be no satisfactory answers.

"A time in every man's, every artist's life," my father continued, "when at the very height of his success he recognizes his incredible, his unbearable failures, when he has no choice but to embrace his incredible, his unbearable failures, and this regardless of the consequences, regardless of what may or may not happen to him. Are you listening to me, Martin?"

I both was and wasn't.

Listening while watching or watching while listening with now the one taking precedence over the other or the other over the one.

"In the end one runs out of excuses, of escapes. In looking back, although looking back is the most dangerous and destructive activity, but in looking back one realizes that all of one's life, one's so-called artistic as well as ordinary life has been nothing but a series of excuses and escapes, listen to me, Martin, all for the sake of survival and so-called security, for getting safely from one day, one year, one decade to the next, and this without ever seriously questioning the reason, any serious questioning would have soon enough revealed that there is none, no, absolutely no discernible reason for getting from one day, one year, one decade to the next, and as for notions of safety, it doesn't take a genius, a true and genuine genius to realize that there is no, absolutely no safety in life, in either our inner or outer lives, there are only excuses and escapes, escapes and excuses, and that those excuses and escapes have led nowhere, accomplished nothing in the end, and then, yes, then perhaps for the first time in one's life one feels utterly alone, utterly defenseless, yes, and facing oneself then, facing one's own nothingness perhaps for the first time in one's life, an incredible, a cleansing feeling, Martin, I highly recommend it, and then in facing oneself, this nothingness in oneself, one is also facing the world, this nothingness of the world, and I'm not talking of despair, Martin, no, this feeling, this state beyond both hope and despair, both hope and despair nothing but further excuses, escapes after all, I just hope you realize, if not now then sometime in the future, one becomes absolutely still then, mirroring, yes, perhaps mirroring nature's absolute stillness, although that stillness beneath the surface of course, beneath the apparently chaotic surface of course, but what I'm trying to tell you is that then there remains nothing to be done, accomplished, or in the nothingness of the end one returns to the nothingness of the beginning, tell me you understand, Martin, just nod if you do."

My father finished his last true, his last genuine work of art.

Even as he spoke, as he lectured he finished his last genuine work of art. The work, the light and colors vibrating in our dimly lit apartment.

My father stopped.

Stood still in front of this last, his most vibrant and vibrating work in light and colors, studied it as though he were studying a stranger's work, a true and genuine artist's work that no longer had anything to do with him.

Courting danger.
Both of us courting, inviting the absolute danger of nothingness in the country.
It was clear from the start, yes, from the very start that neither of us belonged here, neither of us so-called country people although no longer so-called city people, that we were mere visitors in the strictest and most disorienting sense of that term, that our so-called stay in the country was bound to be both limiting and limited, that in the end the specific details of our stay in the country were bound not only to disrupt but destroy our lives, our individual as well as joint lives, that in and through time our very existence was bound to become not only ambivalent, questionable but open to full scale destruction, that it was just sheer chance, pure probability as to which of us would surrender, crack first under the unrelenting and mounting pressure of existence in the country, that the country, nature herself a much more difficult, formidable although in some ways awe-inspiring adversary than the city had ever been, that we, my father and I belonged nowhere then, not to nature, not even to ourselves.
My father held forth, endlessly discoursed about the unbridled cruelty, the wanton destruction of the country, "It's kill or be killed in the country," he often remarked, "nothing but dying and death in the country," the fact that it was the coldest, the most unforgiving winter on record didn't help, "The starkest, the most naked truth finally revealed in the country," he said, "life about nothing but survival or death in the country, the very monotony of life about nothing but survival or death in the country," now and again my father tracing the very origins of art to this brutish and brutal existence in the country, in other words the primeval forests, caves and hunting grounds of the country, "Art about nothing but survival then," he said, "the only true and genuine art of

the time, which may well be the only true and genuine art of all times, all about magic and survival, the use of magic in the fight for survival, self-consciousness, such a thing as the self-consciousness of the so-called modern, civilized artist didn't exist, it simply had no place in this very elemental struggle for survival, the very true and genuine art of the time an intricate part of the very true and genuine struggle for survival, the so-called artists of the time never considered, thought of themselves as artists, magicians perhaps, yes, simply magicians using their magic to survive, and this is why, Martin, their so-called works of art will never be housed in any of our museums, they will forever remain on the walls of caves in the midst of the very elemental struggle for survival, the same now as back then, our various critics, curators and what have you can only marvel at them without in any way touching or collecting them, yes, only the truest and most genuine works of art are beyond touching and collecting, only they inseparable from the lives once lived and strug-gles once fought, my one regret in life, Martin, is that you and I have never traveled to France, to Spain to descend to those caves that house the only true and genuine works of art, to experience, yes, to experience first hand these only true and legitimate works of art, to feel the magic in those only real works of art, nothing of what we know and call art today even comes close, listen to what I'm telling you, Martin, without magic there can be no art just as without art, a certain kind of art, we would know nothing of magic, and magic and a certain kind of art absolutely essential for survival, no longer of course, we have moved beyond any and all absolutes in our modern lives, our so-called existence, our very struggles for survival of an entirely different and relative sort, magic of the purest and most elemental sort has been done away with, outlawed from our cities, the notion of magic and the city antithetical of course, no, magic and cities cannot coexist let alone give birth to one another, only the primeval forests, caves and hunting grounds could have birthed magic, these one and only genuine works of art, just as only magic, these genuine works of art could have birthed those primeval caves, forests and hunting grounds, everything that remains, everything we know of those primeval forests, caves and hunting grounds, the souls, yes, the very souls of those primeval people forever captured in those so-called cave paintings, although their concern was never with history per se, with time per se but only with the present, the ever present moment, the struggles of the present, the ever present moment, our own so-called struggles both absurd and ridiculous compared to theirs, our struggles forever concerned with history, with time and never, hardly ever with the eternal now, by now the eternal now completely beyond our reach, just as life in its most elemental and creative as well as destructive force is also beyond our reach, all of us fractured, fragmented human beings as is reflected in our fractured, fragmented works of art, we now worship only ourselves divorced from the world all around us, whereas those primeval men, those primeval artists worshipped everything about them of which they considered themselves just a part and perhaps not even the most significant part, worship of course a difficult and even dangerous notion, just as magic is a difficult and dangerous notion, but for the truest and most genuine art one must worship everything or nothing, do you understand, Martin, just as one must detect and make use of magic in everything or nothing, we have lost that ability, that sensitivity, but it's there, all there in those cave paintings in Spain and France, the various and countless reproductions hardly do them justice, yes, we live in an age of countless, various and useless reproductions, because we ourselves are nothing but various, countless and useless reproductions the true, the genuine, the real no longer in our art much less in ourselves, or no longer in our art because no longer in ourselves, the challenges in our lives all fake and pseudo challenges and our responses inevitably fake and pseudo responses, yes, and that's why my one regret in life is that we, that you and I have never traveled to Spain, to France, to descend to those caves in Spain and France to confront first hand the only legitimate remnants of the real and genuine in both life and art, instead we moved to the country in a desperate attempt to truly challenge ourselves, but that challenge nowhere near the challenge of those caves in Spain and France, of coming face to face with those wall paintings in the caves of Spain and France."

And so my father.

The frequent litanies, exhortations and prayers of my father.

In spite of our very real need for the most basic items essential to our continued existence in the country, my father refused to walk to the nearest village, those journeys left entirely up to me, my father quite emphatic in his decision, "Never, do you understand, Martin, never will I set foot in a village let alone a city, to once again be led astray by the fake, the pseudo challenges of a village or a city, I would much rather freeze or starve to death in the heart of the country than to once more be confronted by the fake, the pseudo challenges of a village or a city, I no longer wish to have anything to do with the past or the future, Martin, only with the eternal, the ever present, no matter the price, no matter the consequences."

All the same he voiced no objections to my going, so long as he could maintain the fiction of his own so-called real and genuine existence apart from any village or city, any so-called civilized existence that he perceived as a blatant attack on his head as well as his heart.

"You and I are done with all that fakery and flourish," he often told me, "we did not move to the country to perpetuate our false, our second-hand lives."

"Are you unprepared for the unknown, Martin?" my father asked.

A curious if not entirely sensible question.

"In the city it's nothing but preparation," my father continued, "life in the city consisting of nothing but preparation for the next day, week, month or even decade, in other words no day, year or even decade ever fully lived because they serve as mere preparations for the next day, year or even decade, and the preparations always and only for the known, never the unknown, the city strives, does its best to eliminate all the possible unknowns, city life merely moving from one known to the next and the one after, yes, it's only in the country that one fully confronts the unknown, in other words nature at her rawest and most unpredictable self, whether cruel and unforgiving or kind and generous not the issue, no, the unpredictable, the unknown the only issue here, and one can never be prepared for the unknown, listen to me, Martin, the known can only prepare for the known, never the unknown, in other words any and all preparations for the unknown become mere obstacles, stumbling blocks to facing the unknown, anyone moving to the country had best keep this in mind or dismiss it entirely from his mind, primeval man fully and completely recognized this which was why in the end he had to rely on the magic of his true and genuine art, and even though that art too, like all other so-called art, was a fake, a sham, a counterfeit art, because of its intricate relationship to magic it was still a more real and genuine art than any we've managed to produce since, but to be totally unprepared in the face of the unknown is what's called for, the country demanding this complete unpreparedness which very few can accommodate, live with."

In this state of unpreparedness, for what else can I call it, my father went for long walks across the now icy, now snowy fields, he headed in no particular direction but simply followed his instincts, but, no, not even his instincts, only the erratic directions chosen by his legs, he frequently returned from these jaunts, these voyages of undiscovery, his phrase, in excited and feverish states reminiscent of some of his working states during his so-called artistic phase of life, he often mumbled to himself then, "Boundaries," I occasionally heard, "and still the boundaries," he wanted no company on these particular jaunts, these so-called voyages of undiscovery, even his own solitary company something of an obstacle I gathered, a part of the boundaries he tried to demolish, these daytime jaunts, these so-called voyages of undiscovery often traded for nighttime jaunts, so-called nighttime voyages of undiscovery, my father as if both deaf-mute and blind then, "Only the deaf truly hear and the blind truly see," he casually remarked, needless to say I worried for his safety and general well-being, I tried following him but these day and especially his nighttime jaunts impossible to trace, to track, they left no visible trails to follow.

"Nature," my father told me, "yes, the primitive, the elemental forces of nature bent on destruction. The sheer beauty as well as brutality of nature bent on destruction, make no mistake, Martin, naked beauty as destructive as unmitigated brutality, and nature priding herself on both, its brutal beauty as well as beautiful brutality, it cares nothing for our own so-called survival, our insignificant survival, in this it's quite unlike, just the opposite of the city with its fake beauty and sham brutality, the city as if built, constructed for our very survival with both its beauty and brutality hidden beneath the surface and offering no direct challenge to our senses, but survival in the city is just as fake and sham as are its beauty and brutality, in the absence of a direct confrontation the body survives but at the price of the soul's utter destruction, whereas in the country with its stark realities the body is destined to perish while something, yes, something of the soul may yet survive, in other words nature abhors the vacuum of the human soul and would rather destroy the body than to tolerate, to put up with it, this vacuum in the human soul I'm talking of, while the city nurtures and nourishes the body at the price of the soul, in its way the city abhors nothing so much as the true, the genuine human soul, beauty as well as brutality, listen to me, Martin, never camouflaged or faked in the country whereas they are forever faked and camouflaged in the city, and this why we're here, Martin, in case you ever ask yourself, we're here for this direct confrontation with both beauty and brutality, the absolute truth of beauty and brutality that is bound to destroy us in the end, but, no, not before it saves us, saves something of our souls in the process."

I often wondered whether my father himself fully comprehended all the things he was telling me, telling himself, or whether his words, certain of his words and phrases simply took off to birth other words and phrases which in turn birthed still more words and phrases, this seemingly endless cycle nearly impossible to stop once begun, and although I rarely if ever interrupted its flow, I frequently tuned them out, in other words stopped listening, their insidious melodies threatening to overwhelm and possess me, I don't think my father realized the danger, his own words and phrases frequently overwhelming and possessing him as well, and this in spite of his usual and very real mistrust of words, but my father who had by then ceased to be a true and genuine artist substituting words for his light and colors, painting with words instead of light and colors because he simply could not help himself.

"If you want to know, Martin," my father continued, "if you really want to know what it's like being caught in the clutches of the country but not the city, or those of the city but not the country, or, yes, in both, perhaps in both, you have only to picture, to conjure up Munch's 'The Cry,' Munch who throughout his life, his so-called artistic life produced and continued to produce versions of this one painting of his, to go on duplicating this single painting of his, because while Munch himself was no true and genuine artist as everyone including himself sooner or later realized, with this one, this single painting he nevertheless managed to capture something true and genuine, now and again a good and even excellent but by no means true and genuine artist still manages to capture something true and genuine, something of a gift or miracle or pure magic perhaps, an image that once captured will stay with him and his viewers forever, an image that calls for endless repetition both in his subsequent works as well as his viewers' imaginations, just imagine yourself, Martin, a good or even excellent artist who suddenly comes up with, stumbles upon such an image, an image that both summarizes and encapsulates the so-called human condition, although I hate to use such a worn out phrase, but the human condition in both the city and the country let's just say, the very trap and misery of the human condition that exist both in the city as well as the country, the starkest of images about the impossibility of the souls' transmigrations, our souls, you see, with nowhere to go, to migrate just as our bodies with nowhere to migrate, to go, the former forever wedded to, trapped in the latter the same as the latter forever trapped and wedded to the former, and hence the cry, 'The Cry' the only real, the only genuine communication we are capable of in the end, all of us beginning and ending with this sort of cry, yes, just imagine yourself this good and perhaps even excellent artist who suddenly discovers and expresses this most basic universal truth which forever after seizes him the way it seizes his viewers, no, an image such as 'The Cry' simply won't let go, it's the starkest reminder of the impossibility of escapes in either the city or the country, a link, Martin, or perhaps even a return to those primitive images on the cave walls of France and Spain, yes, with a painting like 'The Cry' we come full circle, Martin, return to our origins even as we face our inevitable end, yes, a painting like 'The Cry' is our passport to reality even though it's a pointless and useless passport that allows us to travel nowhere except deep within ourselves."

After this verbal flow, this verbal cascade my father hurried off into the fields, did his best to escape the pull of this image, this 'Cry' resurrected by his verbal flow, his verbal cascade, as so often before it would have been useless to follow, to attempt to catch up with him, my own image of 'The Cry' as if immobilizing me, holding me fast within the walls of the farmhouse.

"There is nothing philosophical about nature," my father told me on his return. "Anyone turning to nature for a so-called philosophy of life will find himself not only betrayed but mocked as well, mocked as well as betrayed, we, you and I, Martin, moved to the country to escape the pull of all ridiculous systems of philosophy, of philosophizing, all systems of philosophy, ridiculous attempts at philosophizing belonging to the city and not the country, just as all so-called art and artifice grounded in the city and not the country, there are few matters of greater consequence than this ending of ridiculous systems of philosophy, of absurd philosophizing, the city would shatter to smithereens, completely self-destruct without its inhabitants' endless philosophizing, city people philosophize in order to escape others as well as themselves, their so-called philosophizing nothing but attempts to escape others and themselves, in other words that which they dare not fully confront in fear of the possible demands it might make on them, the impossible demands it might make on them, country people know nothing of philosophy, of endless philosophizing, they know only direct confrontations with nature's unbridled beauty and brutality, which makes them neither better nor worse than city people, listen to me, Martin, because in the end they too fail to fully confront others as well as themselves, and without such confrontations they never attain their full humanity, their so-called status of true humanity, no, I have as little faith in or hope for city people as I do for country people, or for country people as little as for city people, this is why I insist on my solitary sojourns, my so-called secluded voyages of undiscovery, no, not even you must accompany me, you must make your own sojourns, your own so-called solitary voyages of undiscovery, although in the end I expect nothing to come from this as well except perhaps a final defining and definitive disappearing act, do you understand, Martin, a disappearance, a return to nothingness, to no thingness, Martin, nod if you comprehend, Martin, nod if any of this makes sense to you."

Our farmhouse, our so-called dacha with certain echoes, memories of my father as a young man, a man not yet a true and genuine artist, I was careful not to disturb these, for weeks on end I would move among these echoes of memories or memories of echoes as if trying to orient myself, to find my way, I now and again tried to imagine what it must have been like to attempt to work, to paint in such bleak and barren surroundings, to go about turning oneself into a true and genuine artist in such a bleak and barren space, failing to connect with him now it was simply my way of trying to connect with him in the past, of seeing and even recognizing him before he became a so-called true and genuine artist, from deep beneath the foundations of our farmhouse I now and again touched the ground of these searches or researches, at any rate I felt I did, my father the young man as if hidden beneath layers of earth and dirt, layers of time as it were.

Were we still caught within time then or had my father already begun to move beyond it?

"All art, life itself nothing but negation," my father told me. "You negate the immediate, the obvious to get at something beyond, knowing full well that there may be nothing beyond, that even the possibility of something beyond makes absolutely no sense. We begin with light and colors, start our experiments with light and colors hoping for some sort of explosion, some eventual explosion to move us beyond, yes, even beyond the light and colors themselves. Yet the light and colors all there are, Martin, please, try to understand, in our very experimentations with light and colors we simply move ever deeper into light and colors, anchor ourselves in light and colors, all so-called explosions returning us to light and colors in the end. Never, listen to me, Martin, never do we succeed in moving beyond, in fact we don't even know what moving beyond would, could possibly mean, in other words even though we continue, persist in our work with light and colors we remain in the dark as to its supposed goal, its final aim, light and colors only get us deeper, ever deeper into light and colors but never beyond, are you listening, Martin, never beyond."

My father barely pausing after one train of thought before moving on, going on with the next.

"In the end what is there to comprehend, to understand?"

This after one of his prolonged sojourns, his seemingly endless journeys of undiscovery.

"I raised, I asked myself this question as I was moving across the snowy, the icy fields, the question legitimate, even important perhaps, but as with all legitimate and important questions the answer not to be had or entirely in the negative, the icy, the snowy fields drove this home with an unmistakable clarity, in the end there is nothing to comprehend, to understand although we fool ourselves into thinking that there is, has to be, but in the end life as well as art or art as well as life beyond any real, any true comprehension, it's similar to interpreting our dreams according to some standard which has nothing to do with them, any so-called interpretation of our dreams involves a movement beyond which does nothing more than negate and destroy those dreams, the dreams themselves are their own interpretations, you understand, Martin, there are, there can be no so-called separate interpretations of dreams just as there is, there can be no separate understanding of life, of art, any so-called understanding, comprehension to be found strictly in the living or the various so-called activities of art, none without, we spend much if not most of our lives searching for some sort of outside understanding, some separate comprehension, fool ourselves into settling for now one, now another sort of outside comprehension or understanding, no such thing, Martin, this becomes crystal clear in the end, absolutely clear on a walk through the icy fields of the country, the understanding all within and none without, no, I don't think you appreciate the stark beauty, the sheer simplicity of this, the apparent complexity of life and art reduced to an utter and liberating simplicity in the end, in the end there are no problems to life, to art, so there is no, absolutely no need for any attempts to understand, to comprehend these so-called problems that simply don't exist, they exist in ourselves of course, always and only in ourselves, we ourselves the only creators of problems without the means to solve them, life as well as art without any problems needing to be comprehended, to be solved, there is no need for any sort of understanding in the end, nothingness beyond any and all comprehension, understanding in the end."

My father as if sharing a grand, an all important discovery.

His words perhaps lacking the clarity of his original insight, his discovery, and his very attempt at conveying it fraught with the danger of miscomprehension, but I admired his exhausting effort which carried us beyond evening's falling shadows into night's consuming darkness.

As my father's son and one time imitator I used to view every-thing with a definite beginning, middle and end. Time as linear and not cyclical with endless revisions of revisions. Different now. I now view art as nothing but a series of endless experimentations and life as a series of endless meditations. Or, "We are just a part of the universe's meditations," as my father once put it.

The absence of his artistic activities, his work in light and colors taking its toll on my father. I myself continued with my experiments with dots and lines simply as a way of marking time, of negating the linear while attempting to capture the cyclical nature of time. My father studied these pseudo works of mine without either any encouraging or discouraging comments.

"Yes," he nodded, "yes, reminiscent of Klee in some ways. Klee who set out to reduce and then to explode, first to reduce and then to explode, Klee who in his reductions and subsequent explosions created universes to rival the existing one. Klee satisfied with neither simple destruction nor creation but aiming for a vibrant fusion of both. His work often left me dizzy and gasping for air, although I'm sure nothing could have been further from his original intention, Klee out to create the simplest and therefore most peaceful and calming images, but even peaceful, calming images with ways of exploding in the end, impossible to camouflage, to hide the very vertigo of his imagination from his canvasses. Very often a true, a genuine artist, which Klee undoubtedly was, is after something without his knowing just what, producing for himself a kind of revelation as if after the fact, a kind of discovery in reverse, in other words first the finding and then and only then its subsequent revelation, its discovery, and you may or may not be after the same thing, Martin, in other words first finding and then and only then discovering, but don't let me interrupt, Martin, it's useless to speculate, to hypothesize at this stage of the game."

Art and perhaps life itself become no more than a game to my father by then, a game we were given no choice but to play, in other words a game with no beginning or middle or end.

"The self forever drowning in the self," he said, "playing this game of forever drowning in the self, there is no help from either within or without, the drowning all there is, the only game we're equipped to play."

"Are you familiar with Zen art, with Zen artists, Martin?" my father suddenly asked. "Of course you are. Zen art the non-art par excellence, Martin, just as Zen artists the non-artists par excellence. Ask yourself this, Martin. What is it to observe without the observer, to see without the seer? It takes time of course, days, even weeks of sitting in front of the simplest object, the simplest living thing, a tree, a willow for example, until there is nothing but that tree, that willow in its timeless revelation, and patience is timeless, Martin, it's only with impatience that we are caught, trapped by time, and then as there is only the seeing without the seer, there emerges a painting without the painter, do you understand, Martin, the painting itself quickly, even suddenly accomplished, the tree's, the willow's absolute reality captured in just a few sure lines, all distinctions between reality and the painting as if nonexistent, the painting a non-painting then and the artist a non-artist, only the tree, the willow real, in life as well as in its calligraphic depiction on parchment. Does this mean anything to you, Martin, am I conveying anything at all?"

I wasn't sure.

How could I have been sure at the time?

My father the once true and genuine painter an unknown entity by then. In my mind he had become inseparable from the surrounding countryside, perhaps in his own mind as well, my father as if inhabiting all space and time then, or no space and no time, the difference not at all clear to my mind, my father like an explorer with nothing left to explore, a wanderer with nowhere left to wander, his sojourns, his journeys of undiscovery pushing him to some sort of limit, and beyond that limit the unknown, the unknowable, it was a contest he neither expected nor could possibly win, "No artist, not even the truest and most genuine artist ever won a contest with nature, with himself," he told me, "not even Michelangelo who of all the grand and genuine artists was the greatest fighter of them all, the most remarkable and incredible fighter of them all, but in the end all his undeniable masterpieces nothing but undeniable failures, as remarkable and unforgettable as they were, but Michelangelo's longing for a spaceless space and a timeless time never realized, in the end Michelangelo caught in space and time the same as everyone else."

My father continued in this vein for quite a bit longer, without my knowing just where he was headed.

"All my sojourns, my so-called journeys of undiscovery with but a single or double aim if you will. The search for a spaceless space and a timeless time, our very move to the country with this single and single-minded goal, the discovery of a spaceless space and a timeless time, or rather its undiscovery because such things cannot be discovered but only undiscovered, at best they may discover you, but, no, even that's hoping for too much, such acts of undiscovery must be tainted by neither hope nor hopelessness, they must take you unawares and completely by surprise, beyond, you see, just beyond the edge of the woods I often tell myself, but so far I've merely approached without actually penetrating, something in me still playing for space and time, you understand, Martin, still hesitant about that spaceless space and timeless time hidden in the woods, I am no longer the young man I once was when I last penetrated and somehow survived the encounter, there can be, there will be no survival this time, the young may survive any number of temporary disappearances but not so the old, there can be only one last, one final disappearance in the end, Martin, and after that nothing, nothing must be left behind."

My father no longer with the strength to reinvent himself, his former activities as a true and genuine artist consisted of countless acts of inventions and reinventions, in the country he was no longer willing or capable, I harbored a rational or irrational fear that should he now penetrate the woods it would be for the last and final time, his disappearance as if guaranteed once he penetrated the woods.

"Useless to search, to look for someone," he told me, "who is already lost to himself, who is no longer willing to be found. Please, Martin, please, I don't mean to disturb or upset you, final disappearances of absolutely no consequence in the end, any number of new appearances to take their place, in the end we simply step out of space and time, the only real, the only genuine law of the universe."

My father speaking of life, of art as a tension between the known and the unknown, the knowable and the unknowable.

"While it persists we persist or while we persist it persists, but that tension not infinite, such an infinite tension would be the most absurd and cruel thing imaginable, sooner or later it has to be done with us or we with it, a choiceless conclusion, an ending with no other alternative, we choke on life or life chokes on us, in other words we simply cease to exist, do you understand, Martin, we step out of space and time never to return."

A number, quite a few of my father's works hung in the city's various museums where they both do and don't belong, along with other so-called true and genuine works of art that both do and don't belong there.

I visit them from time to time, telling myself I'm simply visiting my father, an obvious although not entirely useless lie. My father both present and absent from these paintings, the mystery of his final disappearance from life occasionally echoed by the mystery of these works in light and colors.

My relationship with my father now something of a mystery as well that only seems to deepen with the passage of time.

That he is no longer a part of my life and I no longer a part of his is too obvious a truth to require any elaboration. For what sort of a relationship can there be between the dead and the living, the living and the dead?

A well known critic, although not one either liked or respected by my father, recently described my father's works as both comforting and discomforting and categorized his successes as failures and his failures as successes. Perhaps my father would have appreciated such a judgment as mirroring his own.

In a museum nothing is in its proper place. There are no proper places for so-called true, genuine works of art in a museum.

Much against my better judgment I recently participated in a panel discussion about my father's life and works. A ridiculous, a doomed attempt to separate his life from his works, the man from the artist.

"I have been trying to do that all my life, you see," I smiled at one point, "with no more success than we'll have here."

My comment misunderstood. In the ensuing silence my dead father's smile visible only to me.

"In the end the beginning and in the beginning the end," I told them as well.

A certain exhilaration now as I'm working on my father's biography, or anti-biography as my father's biography is quite beyond my capacities and only my own alongside of his within any sort of reach.

Deserting paints and brushes I write now in our old apartment, our so-called studio, substituting words for images in impossible attempts at resurrections. My own more than my father's I suspect. Tackling time itself perhaps without a beginning or a middle or an end. Simply going along for the ride with nothing but time to dictate the pace. A heady blend of certainty and uncertainty frequently interrupted by inner and outer disturbances.

A ridiculous project, chore, an apparently unending work I've imposed on myself. My father's art?

"All of us late arrivals in life," he once told me. "We happen on the scene as if after the fact and do our best to create certainties in the face of overwhelming uncertainties."

My father's presence in his continuing absence or his absence in his so-called continuing presence.

Doing my best to reach the ground, the bottom to all this, which had always been my father's intention as a true and genuine artist. And where he failed or only partially succeeded how can I hope to achieve anything more.

I stick to a strict schedule.

So many hours during the day and so many in the middle of the night.

Or, "'Nothing without discipline and nothing with it,'" as my father once said the Buddha said.

My daytime hours produce one type of biography and the night another with some sort of blending down the road perhaps.

I no longer work as one possessed as I once imagined myself to have done in imitation of my father, in fact I now work with a sort of anti-possession, with neither the material fully possessing me nor I the material. I create distances as I work where I once abhorred distances, again, in imitation of my father.

"No true and genuine artist ever worked without being possessed by his subject and attempting to possess it in turn," my father told me.

I am no true and genuine artist and never have been. All my own so-called works in light and colors nothing but misguided and ultimately failed attempts to connect with my father, to invade his world and avoid being left behind in my own highly uncertain and questionable one.

I am just a word shuffler and procrastinator now, trying to pick up the pieces to see how they would, how they might fit. A constructor of a universe, whether fake or real, that I might yet be able to inhabit.

"The intellect with no place in true and genuine art," my father once told me, "just as the intellect with no place in real life, in genuine living."

I no longer listen to my father the way I once had. I still hear his voice of course, but my own work, my so-called intellectual work in opposition to his non-intellectual one.

My father once in absolute control over his social as well as psychological life, both consciously and unhesitatingly sacrificed to his so-called true and genuine art. Aside from my adherence to schedules in my writing, I exercise no such control over mine, my life the same as it has always been with questions and uncertainties frequently getting the upper hand, the best of me. The most I can claim is a kind of persistence echoing my father's but without his convictions, his inner light as it were.

I mistrust my words even as I jot them down, mistrust my so-called intellectual labor even though it's the only one I seem capable of.

The terms, the very parameters of my father's life still escape me, the way the terms and very parameters of my own life escape me as well.

This work, though, this so-called intellectual work of mine can only take place in the city and not the country, it belongs entirely to the city and not the country, I realized this soon after my father's disappearance, his choiceless disappearance in the country, my abandonment, my solitary existence in the country left me with no resources with which to combat the annihilating force of the country, I could have accomplished no work, let alone the intellectual work I had chosen in the country, no, for that I needed the city's ubiquitous and ever present challenges, to pit myself against the very challenges of the city while challenging myself to accomplish something altogether different, in the country I would have gone to pieces, been destroyed in no time, even disappeared perhaps although in a way entirely different from my father, his disappearance at exactly the right time of his life whereas mine at exactly the wrong one, no, I needed to get back to the city to resume, to continue my struggle with it, just as I needed to get back to my dead father to resume, to continue my struggle with him.

We escape nothing in the end, my father perfectly right about that, we must confront all our routes of escape if only to destroy, to get beyond them, death the only real, the only genuine escape in the end which true and genuine artists recognize more clearly than anyone else, which is why they paint themselves into nothingness in the end, opt for full and total oblivion in the end.

In my so-called writing I'm on a collision course with my father, with the city. A collision with the country would have been an extremely painful and one-sided affair, in other words a foregone conclusion in which I would have been destroyed, made to disappear in no time, just as a collision with my living father, the so-called living true and genuine artist would have been a foregone conclusion as well in which I would have been destroyed and made to disappear in no time, no, nothing could have saved me in such a confrontation, a direct collision, I had to bide my time, wait till after the fact as it were, wait till my father's demise and my own return to the city.

While I have never fancied myself a true and genuine artist, I now occasionally think I might be or eventually become a true and genuine writer, at least so far as my true and genuine confrontation with my dead father and the city is concerned.

The work, my so-called writing takes on a life of its own, several conflicting lives in fact that now lead, pull me in one direction and now in others, during any particular session my father might appear in one guise or disguise while in others during others, the city the same, my difficulties in pinning him down to any particular subject-object or object-subject frequently more than I can handle, any particular vision of him soon enough negated and destroyed as other visions take its place, the city the same, all my attempts to seize and possess soon enough ending in my own seizures and possessions, my dead father escapes my grasp no less than the city all around, my ultimate defeat as if guaranteed from the outset, but it's the very impossibility of this task that keeps me returning to it from one session to the next to the one after.

As a real and genuine artist my father's most significant, perhaps his only genuine relationship to his art, his so-called true and genuine art, even his relationship with me something of an afterthought, at best a relationship between teacher and taught and at worst one between master and acolyte, in my so-called writings I wish to turn the tables, to invent or reinvent my father even as I attempt to invent or reinvent myself.

I struggle with my word-images, my image-words no less than my father struggled with his light and colors, my own experimentations with word-images and image-words in some ways mirroring his one-time experimentations with light and colors. As with every such experimentation the end rarely if ever in sight, or, as my father once put it, "Only the means justify the end, never the end the means."

It occurred to me the other day.

I am playing hide and seek with my dead father now exactly the way I was with the living one, the so-called living true and genuine artist, both of them destined to be forever beyond finding, forever beyond reach, the rules of the game slightly different perhaps but the game itself exactly the same. In other words, he appears in one place only to disappear in another, or disappears in one place only to appear or reappear in another. The ever shifting play of light and colors, never the same, always different.

Or in his presence his absence and in his absence his presence.

'Perhaps I'm intruding,' I frequently tell myself.

My very attempts at comprehension and so a kind of reconciliation nothing more than prolonged acts of intrusion to which I basically have no right, for by what right do the living intrude on the dead when the same living lacked both the determination and the courage to intrude upon the dead when alive, my entire relationship with my father can be summed up by his constant and ongoing challenges to me with the almost entire absence of my challenges to him, my father's entire life lived in the light of constant challenges to himself and so to me, while mine lived in the total absence of challenges to myself and so to him, too late now to reverse the process, to undo what's already been done over our many years of coexistence.

Viewed in this light, my writings nothing more than sheer exercises in futility, ridiculous attempts with no satisfactory goals in sight.

And yet I persist.

'Time plays tricks, Martin,' I tell myself, 'and never will you have a firm grasp of time, a firm grasp of the past in the light of the present.'

And still I persist.

My inner and outer worlds on a collision course as well. In my writings, my so-called anti-biography my inner and outer worlds colliding as well.

In my writings, my so-called anti-biography I come face to face with the unpredictable nature, the uneven passage of time, I only wish I could write a timeless and therefore true and genuine biography or anti-biography, it isn't possible, my very ideas and words consisting of nothing but time itself, my father the same, my dead father consisting of nothing but the uneven, the uncertain past, the uncertain passage of time.

My life consisting now of nothing but my ongoing and frustrating struggles with ideas, with words, something my father would have easily derided and altogether dismissed, punctuated by my now longer, now shorter walks about the city, my now shorter, now longer visits to the city's museums. In some ways my walks, my museum visits as intense as my failed writings, if only to provide the necessary balance between one sort of intensity and another.

"I can't help you," I occasionally hear my father remark, "no, Martin, I can't help you with this."

'The dead with nothing to do with the living,' I tell myself, 'while the living with everything to do with the dead. The living forever seized by the dead,' I tell myself.

It's the same on my visits to the city's museums, my still ongoing encounters with the great and genuine works of art trapped in the city's museums. Drawn to them as if in spite of myself, drawn to them in exactly the same way as I am to my dead father.

I stand defenseless in front of them. I am still the victim of true and genuine art exactly the way I'm still the victim of my dead father, the once true and genuine artist.

Both penetrate me to the core. I seem to lack the vitality, the inner strength with which to resist the force of these true and genuine works of art, just as I appear to lack the vitality, the inner strength with which to resist my dead father, the once true and genuine artist. My father, having been a real and genuine artist himself was well armed against the strength and power of real and genuine works of art. My father forever mirroring true and genuine works of art, just as true and genuine works of art were forever mirroring him. No such mirror ever existed inside me. True and genuine works of art unopposed and unreflected by the vacuum within me.

"Are you prepared, Martin, for Van Gogh, for Gauguin, for Matisse?" my father used to ask.

I wasn't then and am still not now.

For me great and genuine works of art were nothing more than collisions with reality, the very tactile reality of life all around me. For my father those real and genuine works of art constituted reality itself, the only level of reality he was both willing and capable of handling.

My father forever pulling me into his world of true and genuine art while I forever incapable of pulling him into my ordinary, humdrum one.

My father still haunting me along the various corridors and halls of museums without permitting me to haunt him in turn. He leads me to certain works of art then steps back, disappears, abandons me. 'You're on your own, Martin," he whispers, 'you're on your own.'

Now and again I take notes, make certain jottings in front of specific works of art for later use for my work on my father's biography. These prove useless of course. They no more resurrect my feelings at the time I made them than do my often futile attempts to resurrect my dead father.

In spite of the obstacles mentioned above I endlessly return to museums just as I endlessly return to my work on my father's so-called anti-biography. I seem to have no choice in the matter.

"A great and genuine artist works choicelessly," my father once remarked. "His art chooses him and not the other way around."

On several occasions I spent entire nights in museums. Hid in bathrooms until after closing only to emerge later and roam freely in the dark. All light and colors done away with then, my father himself done away with. Great and genuine works of art identified then only by the spaces they occupied. Seeing them darkly then with just the barest outlines as clues to their existence. True and genuine paintings then as if still locked in the minds of true and genuine painters. A simpler way of seeing and experiencing or of not seeing and not experiencing. On those occasions I felt myself the sole possessor of potential worlds, of worlds not yet created. Nothing disturbed me then. Real and genuine works of art as well as my dead father as if suspended in limbo then.

"The potential always greater than the actual," my father once told me.

But it might have been its opposite.

"The actual always greater than the potential," he may have told me.

I no longer recall.

Several so-called publishers interested in my father's anti-biography.

"I'm not a very skilled writer, I'm afraid," I explain to them. "I write strictly for my own amusement and edification."

True or false?

The growing interest in my father's life and work becoming something of an annoying obstacle to my own attempts at unraveling and comprehending. The two as if in diametrical opposition to one another.

Living or dead my father an entirely unsuitable subject for analysis.

"You must comprehend true and genuine works of art all at once, Martin, or not at all."

Does the same apply to him?

Comprehension must occur all at once or not at all, that is without any prior preparation, without even words perhaps.

And.

Looked at a certain way, my writing, my continuing work on my father's anti-biography has been nothing but preparation, an obstacle to a sudden and therefore encompassing comprehension.

"There can be no preparations for life," my father once told me, "just as there can be no preparations for comprehending great and genuine works of art. All preparations for life become mere substitutes for living, just as all preparations for comprehending genuine works of art become mere substitutes for actual comprehension."

The teasing, the fragmented bits of understanding never turn into a satisfying whole. My father would have been amused by my efforts to capture him piecemeal, to possess him through words.

It's an unsettling realization.

'The city getting the better of you, Martin,' I hear him saying. 'Your words not strong enough to withstand the assaults of the city, of time itself. You must find another way.'

My father right about one thing.

In the end nothing fails like success nor succeeds like failure.

In the end I abandon my failed attempts at my father's so-called anti-biography at exactly the same time as I decide to move beyond true and genuine works of art.

I have no idea what will become of me.

"Artists," my father once told me, "true and genuine artists never concerned with immediate appearances. Their only involvement with creative misunderstandings."

Reality bound to overwhelm me in the end.

How will I face my father's so-called immediate appearances without his, others' and my own creative misunderstandings.

Without art I will no doubt die of the truth as Nietzsche predicted.

The same as my father perhaps?

Without art's mitigating role my closeness to reality will no doubt become unbearable.

I make plans, tentative plans for my survival.

I'll travel to Spain, to France, descend to the prehistoric caves of Spain and France.

The undertaking not without its obvious difficulties as well as inherent dangers.

I am a poor planner by nature and even worse at carrying out whatever I've planned in advance. Any number of necessary details escape my attention, even a single one of which may be sufficient to derail my journey. In addition to which I'm an inferior traveler, my travels of the mind, the imagination much more readily accomplished than those in actuality.

And as to the caves themselves.

Who is to say I'll ascend once I've descended, that I'll somehow overcome the pull of that ancient world once it has me in its grips?

My father's last, his final penetration into the woods comes to mind.

"Are you ready for oblivion, Martin?" he once asked.

Still, that journey to the prehistoric past may be unavoidable, a wordless, perhaps even timeless past where life and art and magic fused into the only comprehensible whole I know.

There are disappearances and disappearances, I tell myself and a disappearance into those timeless caves, the very origins of art highly preferable to any other I can imagine.

I set the journey into motion.

Make the necessary calls, passport, tickets and so forth.

I won't look at another true and genuine work of art or entertain another thought of my father, the once true and genuine artist until I will have arrived at the very source of life and magic and art.

As for my emergence afterwards?

No, I can't be bothered with that now.

In my father's words I'm unprepared for the unknown.

He would have been pleased, I think.